Discard

camp CONFIDENTIAL

RSVP

GROSSET & DUNLAP
Published by the Penguin Group
Penguin Group (USA) Inc., 375 Hudson Street,
New York, New York 10014, U.S.A.
Penguin Group (Canada), 10 Alcorn Avenue, Toronto, Ontario, Canada M4V 3B2
(a division of Pearson Penguin Canada Inc.)
Penguin Books Ltd, 80 Strand, London WC2R ORL, England
Penguin Ireland, 25 St Stephen's Green, Dublin 2, Ireland
(a division of Penguin Books Ltd)
Penguin Group (Australia), 250 Camberwell Road, Camberwell, Victoria 3124,
Australia (a division of Pearson Australia Group Pty Ltd)
Penguin Books India Pvt Ltd, 11 Community Centre, Panchsheel Park,
New Delhi - 110 017, India
Penguin Group (NZ), Cnr Airborne and Rosedale Roads, Albany, Auckland 1310,
New Zealand (a division of Pearson New Zealand Ltd)
Penguin Books (South Africa) (Pty) Ltd, 24 Sturdee Avenue, Rosebank,
Johannesburg 2196, South Africa

Penguin Books Ltd, Registered Offices:
80 Strand, London WC2R ORL, England

Library of Congress Control Number: 2005016660

ISBN 0-448-43962-X   10 9 8 7 6 5 4

camp
CONFIDENTIAL

RSVP

by Melissa J. Morgan

Grosset & Dunlap

Calling all Camp Lakeview Campers!

You are cordially invited to the
Annual Camp Lakeview Reunion!

When: Saturday, February 19th,
5 to 10 P.M.

Where: Village Bowl,
Greenwich Village, NYC

Why: To share Camp Lakeview memories
and make new ones!

Who: YOU, of course!
It won't be a party without you!

Dear Lakeview Alumni,

Can you believe that six months have passed since summer's end at Camp Lakeview? We didn't want to wait until next June to see all of you again, so we're throwing a campwide reunion party at Village Bowl! Village Bowl is a retro-stylin' four-story bowling complex in the heart of Greenwich Village. There will be lots of activities, great food, friendship, and fun!

Join us beneath twirling disco balls for glow-in-the-dark bowling. Play video games and shoot pool in a room furnished with inflatable chairs and sofas. The Lanetown Screening Room will feature an advanced screening of the new animated film *Deep Sea Diary*, featuring the voices of Brad James and Josie McLaughlan. We'll dance to KMAXXX, NYC's hottest DJ; and Dr. Steve himself will wave the checkered flag at the underground go-kart racetrack!

We will provide heaps of burgers, fries, pizza, and sodas. And of course each bunk will load up their bunk table with yummy treats and cool decorations! See your enclosed contact sheet for the Camp Lakeview e-mail addresses for your counselors and CITs, plus all the details about how to get to Village Bowl, shoe rentals, attire, and more.

RSVP soon, please, so we can make sure we have plenty of food and fun waiting for you. We will SPARE no effort to get on our GAME. We really hope to see each and every one of you at the Camp Lakeview "BOWL-DOWN"!

Cordially,
Your Lakeview Staff

chapter
ONE

"More bagel, Nat, fewer lists, please," Natalie Goode's mother said. They had stopped at Mavin Deli on the way to Natalie's school for tasty cranberry-walnut bagels slathered with cream cheese.

"Okay, Mom," Natalie said, glancing up to see that her mom was still reading the *New York Times*.

Shifting in her chair, Natalie got back to business—the business of organizing the best reunion party weekend in the history of Camp Lakeview.

If we go to a movie, we can buy treats there. So I won't have to plan for too much food at our place afterward. But which movie should we go to? Hey, where's my movie list?

She shuffled her papers like a pack of cards as she searched for her spreadsheet of movie possibilities. A whoosh of moist, cold air buoyed the errant page as the front door opened for a large crowd of businessmen, stamping the snow and ice off their shoes and brushing the sleeves of their heavy wool coats. Natalie grabbed the black paper before it could fall to the floor, which was damp with melted snow.

"Nat," her mother said again, looking up from

the newspaper. Steam rose from the coffee cup in her right hand. *"Eat. Please."*

"But I have so many things to do before Friday!" Natalie insisted. She pulled another piece of paper from her stack titled *RVSPs for FRIDAY SLEEPOVER* and read down the list of names: *Alyssa, Grace, Jenna. With me, that's four. They'll have been traveling. They'll probably be really hungry.*

"How many pizzas should I order for Friday night?" she asked her mother. "Do you think Alyssa likes anchovies? I'll bet she does. It's so weird that I spent eight weeks in the same bunk with her and I have no idea if she likes anchovies."

"That's a stumper," her mother teased her. "Since I've never met Alyssa."

"She's artsy," Natalie told her. Her face lit up. "And *you're* artsy. And *you* like anchovies."

"Yes, but I'm an art *buyer*," her mother replied, tipping her coffee cup toward her mouth. "Not an artist *per se*." She cocked her head as she considered the possibilities. "Is Alyssa an artist, an art patron, or—"

Natalie chuckled as the answer popped into her head. "She's a vegetarian. And anchovies are *fish*."

"Only technically," her mother said drily.

Natalie's mother went back to sipping her coffee and glancing down at the *Times*. She wore a very cool bracelet of seven hand-carved cameos—profiles in white of ladies with their hair swept up in ringlets—set in lovely, apricot-colored stone. She had bought the bracelet during her summer art-buying trip to Europe.

"I'll order three extra-large pizzas," Natalie said finally. "We can always have the cold leftovers for breakfast."

"True," her mom said, amused. Cold pizza had been one of Natalie's favorite breakfasts ever since she was seven, when she had spent a summer with her father in Rome during one of his movie shoots.

Natalie's dad was the international movie superstar Tad Maxwell, a fact she had tried hard to hide from her bunkmates at Camp Lakeview. He and Natalie's mom had split up when Natalie was four, and he wasn't around much because of his busy career.

But the girls of Bunk 3C had discovered her secret soon enough, when he had showed up in a limo with his personal assistant, his bodyguard, and his gorgeous girlfriend, Josie McLaughlan. That was the reason her new animated movie was going to be shown at the reunion. Some of the campers had never gotten over their shock and awe, but Natalie's best buds liked Natalie just for Natalie.

So I really need to make sure they have a great time. They're such great friends.

"Okay, on to soda," Natalie announced. "We have to be sure to get some diet, because Alex can't drink that much sugar. I wonder if the girls like egg creams. We could go to that new restaurant over by Lincoln Center. Or is that just a New York thing?" She wrinkled her brow. "Maybe I should e-mail them all to find out." She reached for her backpack to retrieve her cell phone. "What time is it? I could start calling—"

"Whoa, honey, slow down!" her mother urged. "The whole point of a reunion is to see your friends again and have fun together. Not drive yourself crazy worrying over every little detail of your preparation."

Natalie put the backpack down. She knew she was right. Her mom gave lots of parties and she attended even more. Natalie had heard many stories of parties gone terribly wrong because the host or hostess was just too worn out to relax and mingle.

It *was* going to be superfun seeing all her bunkmates again. But Natalie couldn't control her nervousness. She knew she had to make some plans. In addition to the official campwide reunion at Village Bowl, Natalie was playing hostess at not one but *two* sleepovers.

The first one would be smaller, with just Alyssa, Grace, and Jenna, who would stay over all day Saturday. Her mother had already made arrangements for them to have a spa day, but that wouldn't take up all the time they had together. And there was still breakfast and lunch to work out. Then getting ready for the party.

Then after the party at Village Bowl, the whole bunk was coming over for a second sleepover. That meant that all eleven of her bunkmates would be spending the entire night in her apartment! And most of them would be hanging out until early Sunday afternoon. And *that* made her supernervous.

I've been nervous around these girls before, though, and things have worked out.

She thought back to her first day at Camp Lakeview, a summer camp in rural Pennsylvania. She had been very skeptical that anything good would come of her mother's decision to send her there. Natalie's mom wanted Natalie to broaden her horizons, which apparently included the horizon of "nature"—while she traveled all over Europe, buying art for her gallery.

As far as Natalie had been concerned, nature appeared to consist of the bug-infested, poison-ivy-laden wilds of Far Meadow and the mysterious waters of the lake for which the camp was named. And nature had been heavily populated: there were more kids at Camp Lakeview than students in all the grades of Natalie's private school back in the city.

Natalie had spent the first couple days of camp yearning for the familiar skyscrapers of the concrete jungle she called home. She'd missed her soft bed, her immaculate bathroom, and most of all, her privacy.

Then she had grown to love Camp Lakeview, with its mosquitoes, poison ivy, and especially her eleven sometimes-irritating, sometimes-quirky bunkmates. She'd even trekked her way back to the overnight camp in the wilderness when Chelsea had run after that rabbit. Simon had bragged about her to everyone, like she was some kind of fearless trail guide.

Yes, it had taken her a while to settle in, but by the time summer was over and she was due to come home, it was difficult for her to believe that she hadn't been a Lakeview camper for years.

Six months had passed since the end of camp. She was back in the greatest city of the world, in her second semester of sixth grade, and doing lots of fun things with Hannah, her best New York friend. It seemed a lifetime ago that she had shared Jenna's care packages of chocolate-on-chocolate cupcakes, and applauded Grace and Brynn in the campwide production of *Peter Pan*.

At the thought of seeing the girls of Bunk 3C again, her stomach fluttered with anxiety. Although she had many fond memories of them, she figured they had changed a lot since they'd seen one another. It would almost be like getting to know eleven new people—but with the added responsibility of making sure they had a fun weekend.

On top of that, she was going to see Simon again. Simply planning what to wear to dazzle him was almost more than she could handle from now until the party.

Her mother interrupted her thoughts. "Sweetie, it's just pizza and a movie, and your good friends in sleeping bags. Nothing to be worried about."

Can she read my mind? Or am I that obvious? Natalie smiled at her mother, knowing she meant well. But her stomach still fluttered. Because it was much, much more than that.

They're coming to my city and staying in my home. What if they don't like the food, or the movie, or any of the activities I've planned? What if they think I've ruined the reunion for them? I don't have a whole summer for them to get used to my world the way I got used to theirs.

"Oh, look at the time!" her mother cried, glancing down at her watch. "If we don't leave now, you'll be late for school." They both loved to walk to Natalie's school whenever they had time.

She folded up the *Times* and took a last sip of her coffee as Natalie gathered up her lists. They both pushed back their chairs, Natalie bobbing her head at Mr. Edelman, the deli owner, as he waved good-bye.

They went to the coat rack and retrieved their coats, Natalie handing her mother her stack of papers so she could slip her arms through the sleeves of her fabulous new leather coat from Paris.

"Goodness, you have a lot of lists," her mom said as she neatened up the pile. "Maybe we could put this all in a notebook tonight."

"That's a great idea," Natalie said enthusiastically, taking the papers back while her mom put on her own coat.

Just as they walked onto the sidewalk, a sharp gust of wind caught Natalie by surprise. Her papers flew out of her arms. They capered and cartwheeled and flapped away like black crows against the snowy landscape.

"Oh, no!" Natalie cried, racing after the closest few. She bent down and retrieved three pages from a snowdrift piled around the base of a fire hydrant.

Natalie rose to her feet, facing the traffic as honking taxis and a heavily bundled bicycle messenger rolled over at least half a dozen more of her carefully thought-out lists.

"Oh, great," she moaned. "I'll have to start over!"

"No, sweetie," her mother insisted, gesturing for her to move along. "Think back. Haven't some of the best times with your friends been spent just hanging out? Give your weekend with your friends room for some surprises."

"Oh, I'm sure we'll have a few of those," Natalie said glumly. Then she chuckled. "After all, Jenna will be there. And Grace, too." That meant pranks for sure. She just hoped she was up for them.

"There, you see?" Her mom walked behind Natalie and retrieved another piece of Natalie's black paper, which had flapped against a tree trunk. It was the RSVP list for Saturday's all-bunk sleepover. Most of the names were smeared from the wet snow, but the name she could read most clearly made her lose her smile.

For while it was true that fun-loving Grace and Jenna would be there, and her best camp friend Alyssa, too, it was also true that the biggest party-pooper of Camp Lakeview had let her know just yesterday that she would be there, too.

Chelsea.

Chelsea wasn't joining them until Saturday—her mom had to work late on Friday and her father couldn't drive right now—but Chelsea would eventually be there. And she could be so sour and cranky . . . it was going to be an extra challenge to be nice to her.

I'm glad we're making that surprise for her, Natalie thought. *Maybe it will de-crankify her.*

"Sweetie? Stop worrying," her mother said, interrupting her thoughts.

"Okay, Mom," Natalie replied.

Just show me where the worry off-switch is, and I will!

chapter

TWO

"Paging Mia Hamm!" Alex Kim's mother called from the barely open sliding glass door that led to the backyard.

"On my way!" Alex called back.

Alex wore thick leggings and a heavy hockey sweater as she dribbled her soccer ball across the brittle brown grass in the backyard. As she panted, her breath curled upward like smoke.

She had been practicing since dawn. She needed to drastically improve her game by next Saturday. She was playing indoor soccer for the Blue Angels. Last Saturday, with both teams tied, she had lost control of the ball, and the Maroon Menace, their rivals for the league championship, scored a goal in the last eight seconds of play.

That game would have been ours, if I hadn't messed up, Alex thought, angry at herself for her sloppy dribbling skills.

The sliding glass back door opened farther, to reveal Alex's petite mother in a cream-colored velour track suit and pink Uggs, holding a jade-green bowl in both hands. Her black hair was pulled back in a ponytail that bounced when she talked.

"Alex, you know you need to eat," she admonished her daughter. "Take extra-good care of yourself, sweetheart. You have a big weekend ahead of you."

Alex sighed as she untied her cleats and slung them over her shoulder. Ever since her parents had learned how Alex had fallen into diabetic shock at camp—brought on by eating sugar-laden Twinkies and on top of that, neglecting to take her insulin—they had hovered around Alex like she was two years old.

She came into the warm house and sat at the dining room table. A bowl of steaming oatmeal was waiting for her. Picking up her spoon, she sampled it, and instantly detected the artificial sweetener her mom had used. Wistfully, she remembered the rivers of maple syrup she used to drown her hot cereal in before she was diagnosed. She could still have honey on occasion, but the days of maxing out on sugar and syrup like her friends did were definitely over.

Meanwhile, her mom had resumed cutting mounds of colorful vegetables for Alex's mid-morning school snack.

Her mom said, "Be sure to take the new batch of insulin needles to practice this afternoon."

"I will," Alex replied. For each activity she was engaged in, she had to provide an insulin kit for the coach. She had hopes of switching to insulin pills she could take by mouth, or maybe even an insulin pump, but for now, her usual dosage was one injection a day.

She also wore a silver medical I.D. bracelet. That would alert people to her condition if she couldn't speak for herself. She had been very lucky that Julie, her Lakeview counselor, had known what to do after Alex collapsed at camp. But without reading the warnings on her bracelet, an unknowing stranger might not interpret Alex's dizziness and confusion as symptoms of her blood-sugar imbalance. With the wrong emergency care, Alex could wind up going into a diabetic coma . . . or worse.

"We need to leave for school soon," her mother told her as she quickly packed the vegetables into a bright blue snack container.

"Okay, Mom." Alex took the snack container from the counter. She hoisted up her heavy school backpack from the floor so she could load it in. She unzipped the main compartment and pulled out her Firefly cell phone.

A text message winked in the window of the face-plate, which was decorated with sparkly soccer balls:

CU soon! B.

She grinned. "B" was Brynn, her bestest bud from camp. Brynn was coming to spend the night on Friday. Alex's game was bright and early on Saturday morning. As soon as it was over, the two girls would get ready for the reunion together and take the bus into New York City.

When she'd first received the official Camp Lakeview invitation to the reunion, Alex had been nothing but excited. Then things got complicated—Natalie Goode invited her to spend the night at her apartment on Friday. Coolness, except that was the night before her next soccer game. And since she had essentially lost the last one for her team, she knew she had to show.

Not realizing Alex's dilemma, Natalie had described in excruciating you-cannot-miss-this detail all the fun activities she had planned for her guests. A movie at a local theater, and a spa day where everyone could have manicures, pedicures, and facials. Alex had wanted like anything to go.

But she had a commitment to her team. And with their standings hanging in the balance of this Saturday's game—after she herself had handed the victory to the Maroon Menace—she knew she couldn't skip the Saturday morning game.

She had been very disappointed. But as her mother had pointed out, she would still be able to stay over at Natalie's all-bunk sleepover on Saturday, after the party at Village Bowl.

"You can still be a good team member *and* have fun with your bunk," her mother had said.

So she made her decision: skip Friday night at Natalie's and play the game on Saturday. The rest of the Blue Angels were very envious that she was going to Village Bowl—but even *more* impressed that she knew Tad Maxwell's daughter, and would be spending the night at her fancy penthouse apartment.

Then the trouble started. Like the other girls of Bunk 3C, Alex had been posting her ideas about how to decorate their party table on the bunk blog that Julie, their counselor, had created. Everyone had loved Alex's idea of using a blue-and-red Color War theme.

Excited, Alex had hurried out to buy some table-cloths and napkins, using some of her birthday money from her grandmother. And she worked out what she thought was a pretty cool outfit, mixing one of her standard navy polo shirts with khaki pants and red accessories—a red scrunchie and a necklace of red crystal beads.

But the very next day, Natalie posted that she had learned that Bunk 3A was going with the Color War theme as well. Natalie had insisted that since 3A were 3C's traditional rivals, they couldn't possibly use the same theme. When Alex had posted, "Y not?" Natalie had simply replied, "Puh-leeze!"

Natalie went on to suggest they "be more subtle" by mixing blue and red together, to come up with a purple color scheme. The entire bunk got on board with that and Julie announced that it was official. Before the end of that same day, Natalie had posted an entire list of purple stuff they could buy and websites to order it all online. Julie thanked her for being such a huge help. So did everyone else.

Except Alex. Alex was really mad. Natalie had taken over the whole thing!

Frustrated, Alex put all the napkins and tablecloths she had purchased back in their sack so she could return them . . . only to trip in the parking lot of the party store and dump everything into a pothole filled with melting, dirty ice. Two packages of napkins were ruined . . . and the party store clerk refused to refund her money for them.

Meanwhile, Natalie kept coming up with more and more plans . . . down to the point of assigning each girl what kind of treats to bring. Finally Julie logged in and said that it would probably be easier just to let everyone contribute a surprise.

To make matters worse, Alex's mother started fretting about Alex going so far away. Alex couldn't believe what she was hearing. After all, she was in competitive soccer and her teams traveled all over the place. True, her mom usually accompanied the team as a chaperone, but *still.*

She complained to Brynn about it, and it turned out that Brynn's mother was also a little anxious about Brynn traveling to New York City by herself. So somehow, it got decided that Brynn would stay over at Alex's on Friday, and the two would go to New York together.

"A perfect solution!" Brynn had declared.

For me, anyway, Alex thought. *But does Brynn really want to stay here? I'd give anything to go to Natalie's on Friday. Or at least I would have, before she started running everything. But Brynn doesn't have any issues with Natalie.*

"We're going to have so much fun!" Brynn had added. "I can't wait to see all your trophies and eat your mom's Korean barbecue!"

Alex was only semi-convinced. How much fun could they really have when the start time for her Saturday morning game was eight o'clock? Especially given that because of her diabetes, she would have to go to bed super-extra-early?

Just like in soccer, I'll do what it takes to make sure Brynn enjoys herself while she's here. Only I sure hope I don't fumble the ball.

Then we'll go to the reunion at Village Bowl and I will totally not let Natalie's bossiness ruin my good time!

▲ ▲ ▲

Propped up in bed with his favorite pillows, Chelsea's dad examined her invitation to the Camp Lakeview reunion and said, "Are you getting excited about seeing your old friends, Chelse?"

Chelsea hesitated. She felt terrible thinking about having a good time when her dad looked so pale and tired. His hair, light blond like Chelsea's, was starting to thin. Soon it would fall out. She knew the routine; they'd all gone through this before.

Her mom, walking into the bedroom with a folded stack of laundry, looked almost as worn out as Chelsea's dad. Her father had just started a new round of chemotherapy for his cancer, and she knew they both were exhausted with worry.

I'm really worried, too.

Both her parents smiled at her, waiting for her answer.

"I don't know," she said uncertainly, as she perched on the side of the bed. Her dad took his hand in hers. His fingers were very bony. "I'm starting to think about not going. Those girls are going boy crazy. That's all they e-mail about anymore. And they're so silly. All they do is read links to fashion magazines and news about movie stars." She flushed. "I mean, movie stars besides Natalie's dad. It's okay to read about him, I guess. Since he *is* her dad."

Her mom opened up a drawer in the double bureau and laid in some white T-shirts. "Sometimes silly is good," she said, as she shut the drawer and leaned against it. "I remember having all kinds of fun at sleepovers when I was your age."

Chelsea almost said, "Poor Mom, you're sure not having much fun now," but she kept her mouth pursed in a straight line.

Since her father's illness, so much had changed. Chelsea didn't go to boarding school anymore. She lived at home with her parents and her sister. Her sister spent most of her time hanging out with her own friends—she had already left for school with a big crowd—and Chelsea couldn't understand how she could have fun when their dad was so sick.

Her father studied her. "Are you having second thoughts? You don't have to go, but I have to admit I'm puzzled by your lack of enthusiasm. You came home from camp with all kinds of great stories about your summer."

"Yeah, I had a really great time," Chelsea blurted. Then she took a breath and quickly added, "But I've changed since then. After all, it's been six months since the end of camp. A lot can happen in six months."

Her parents exchanged a look. Chelsea was used to those looks, and she knew what this one meant. They thought she was talking about her father's cancer. After two years of good test results, his disease had come back in September, and it had gotten worse since then.

Chelsea's mom said, "Well, we can talk about it on the way to school. We have to go now, or you'll be late. Give Daddy a kiss."

She carefully kissed his hollow cheek.

She stood, picked up her invitation, and placed it on the nightstand, next to her father's amber-colored bottles of pills and a big box of tissues.

They put on their heavy winter outerwear at the front door. Chelsea slipped on a pair of mittens she had gotten for Christmas. Then she picked up her backpack.

Her mother put on her gloves. Then they went out the front door, her mom first, into a flurry of snowflakes. As they hurried to their SUV, her mom stopped in the middle of the driveway. She tipped back her head and stuck out her tongue. Chelsea burst out with a giggle and said, "Mom!"

"Mmm! Cherry-flavored snow! We're getting our own private snow cones! Try it, Chelsea!" her mother urged her. "Oh, my gosh, it's root beer now!"

"Oh, Mom," Chelsea said, laughing. "You're so crazy!"

"My mistake! They're Skittles!" her mom cried. "Chelsea, we're in a Skittles commercial!"

With a big guffaw, Chelsea stopped walking, too. The hood of her jacket fell back as she lifted her chin, imitating her mother. The two of them stood in the falling snow, shouting out flavors:

"Lime!"

"Grape!"

"Sour apple!"

"Bubble gum!"

By the time they got in the car to drive to school, their faces were half-frozen. Chelsea experimentally touched her cheeks and sighed with contentment as the heater began to defrost her chin and nose.

The houses and trees were covered with snow, creating a beautiful winter wonderland. Chelsea's mom said, "It would be fun to see New York like this, Chelsea. Maybe you girls will go skating at Rockefeller Center. Are ice skates on Natalie's list of things to bring?"

"I don't remember," Chelsea replied. "She had a lot of lists." The envelope containing the invitation from Natalie was about twice as thick as the one from Camp Lakeview, even counting the map to Village Bowl *and* the RSVP card and envelope that had been enclosed.

Her mother smiled. "Natalie's working hard to

make sure you have a good time. I'm sure she's cooked up all sorts of exciting things for you to do."

Chelsea shifted uncomfortably. She knew her mom was trying to make it easy to talk about the weekend, but Chelsea still felt funny discussing it.

"Mom, I know you want me to go," she said. "But those girls are different from me. They're really immature. I probably wouldn't have a very good time."

Her mom braked at the red light on Emerson Street. Chelsea's school was only two blocks away. She was glad. She wanted to get out of the car so they wouldn't have to talk about this anymore.

"I thought you wanted to go back to Camp Lakeview this summer," her mom reminded her. "Some of those girls will probably be your bunkmates again. It seems like it would be fun to catch up and see what's been happening with them before next June."

"Maybe I won't go this summer after all," Chelsea said, before she had really thought through what she was about to say. She caught her breath. *Not go to camp?* Then she shrugged. "Maybe I'll stay home. I could even get a job!"

Her mom tousled her hair. "A twelve-year-old with a job?"

"Sure. So I could, you know, make money," Chelsea said excitedly, imagining herself behind a cash register at Limited Too at the mall. Or maybe she could work for Mr. Markham, who owned a dog grooming business. She'd love to bathe frisky little puppies and give poodles fancy haircuts!

"What do you need money for, Chelse?" her mom asked, her expression growing more serious.

"Oh, you know, to help out." She shrugged her shoulders, wondering if she had suggested something that was wrong. Her mom had such an odd look on her face. Was she angry? "So you guys don't have to worry so much."

"We aren't worried," her mom assured her. She reached out and brushed a tendril of hair away from Chelsea's forehead. "Well, we're a little concerned. But that's something for *us* to worry about, sweetie. Not you. Everything is going to work out. Just have a little faith."

Suddenly Chelsea felt like crying. She didn't really know why. Her moods went up, then plummeted like the waterslides at Wet World. It seemed she never knew how she was going to feel from one moment to the next.

"Okay, Mom, I'll have faith," she promised. She nodded and smiled at her, and then she looked out the window. At this time on weekday mornings, the streets were always clogged with SUVs and minivans brimming with kids. It was pretty much a madhouse, and Chelsea almost envied the students who lived far enough away to take the bus. The last bus she had ridden had been the one home from camp, and it was fun to participate in the laughter and singing. She'd even listened to one girl's iPod for over an hour.

Their SUV pulled up to the curb. As she gathered up her backpack, Chelsea spotted her new friend Belle in the distance. Underneath her signature pink-on-pink backpack, she had on a thick, fleecy parka of dark orange and white. Chelsea thought it looked totally hot. That exact shade of jack-o'-lantern orange was currently Chelsea's favorite color.

Belle's curly dark brown hair tumbled around her shoulders from beneath a black-and-silver knitted cap. A silver yarn pom-pom dangled from a woven braid extending from the cap's crown, bobbing as Belle moved with the crowd toward the school's front doors.

Chelsea wanted to catch up to her, so she pushed on the door handle and popped the door open as she prepared to carefully climb down onto the slippery ice.

"Gotta hustle," she said to her mom. "I want to walk with Belle."

"It's so nice that you two are friends. You know," her mother said thoughtfully as Chelsea slung her right leg onto the step of the SUV, "your father and I haven't had a weekend alone since you went to Belle's sleepover. That was over a month ago. Your sister's going to spend the weekend at Jessie Greenfield's house. You would kind of be doing us a favor by going to New York."

"Oh, *Mom*," Chelsea said, covering her mouth in astonishment. "You guys are so weird."

Her mother chuckled. "We may be weird, but it would be fun to watch a movie with a PG-13 rating and have some Greek takeout." Chelsea didn't care for Greek food. Most of it tasted sour to her.

Then her mom's tone changed. "Chelse, we're both proud of you for trying so hard to help the family. But really, sweetie, you don't *need* to try so hard."

She's just saying that, Chelsea decided, as she eased down onto the icy sidewalk, planting one foot firmly beneath herself. *They really do need my help.*

"Okay, Mom," she said.

"It's just one night," her mom added.

"Right."

Chelsea shut the door and stood back as the SUV rolled away and joined the long, winding parade of parents dropping off their kids.

She minced with tiny steps on the slippery ice, melting into the jostling crowd of heavily clothed middle school students rushing to class.

"Belle!" she called, hurrying after her friend, but taking care not to slip.

"Hey," Belle said, turning to wait for her. Collin walked on ahead without even looking back at Belle. That was a potentially good sign that they weren't *hanging out*, hanging out. It was hard enough for Belle to fit Chelsea into her busy schedule—she had indoor soccer, chorus, Girl Scouts, and karate.

"What's up?" Belle asked her. "You look kind of freaked out."

"I do not," Chelsea snapped.

"Sorry," Belle said. "I thought maybe you had been crying."

"No way! I have the most awesome weekend planned. I'm going to a sleepover in Manhattan with Tad Maxwell's daughter."

Belle's eyes grew huge. "Oh, my gosh! You mean your camp friend, Natalie? Wow, Chelsea, that is awesome!" She shook her head in amazement. "You are totally the luckiest girl I know!"

"I know," Chelsea said, grinning at her.

But the thing was, she didn't feel very lucky.

And she still wasn't sure if she wanted to go.

chapter
THREE

"There they are!" Natalie screamed, jumping up and down beside her mother.

They stood shoulder-to-shoulder in the main terminal of the busy, noisy bus depot as Grace and Alyssa's bus from New Jersey lumbered slowly into view along the snow-covered blacktop. Snow flurried in the black sky; the sun had gone down about half an hour before.

As Natalie pushed open the glass double doors, the air brakes made a sighing sound that overpowered her mother's response.

"Grace! Alyssa!" Natalie cried, waving both arms as she trotted toward the bus.

"Stay back, miss," a burly uniformed security guard ordered her, blocking Natalie's way. "Please wait for your party behind the yellow line."

Natalie obeyed, eagerly scanning the heavily bundled passengers as they descended the bus steps and walked toward the terminal. *Too old, too tall, too not-them, too—*

Alyssa appeared first, beaming at Natalie as she stepped through the bus's door. She gave her a happy wave.

Trust Lyss to dress in style, Natalie thought fondly. Her friend had on a black wool duster with big shoulders and a black beret. And was she wearing a ton of makeup! Her hair—back to black after the Ronald McDonald dye job last summer—was braided into a thick rope that trailed over her left shoulder. Ornate, dramatic chandelier earrings and a purple-and-black fringe scarf completed her outfit. Natalie bet she had on a cool black T-shirt splattered with paint underneath her coat.

And there was Grace behind her!

"Gracie!" Natalie cried.

"Lookin' good, Goode!" Grace yelled, giving her a thumbs-up. She was wearing a pair of jeans, red high tops, and a brown-and-red-leather jacket that said NEW JERSEY DEVILS across the back. Her crazy red curls were held back in place with pink-and-red beaded barrettes.

The two girls hopped down the rest of the steps, Grace waving her hands like a wacky windmill. Natalie held out her arms for both of them. Alyssa hurried toward her; Grace laughed and jogged around her to get there first.

"You guys are here!" Natalie cried, as first Grace and then Alyssa hugged her tightly. She hadn't realized how much she missed them until this moment. Grace, Alyssa, and Natalie, together again at last!

"We are gonna have a blast!" Natalie told them. "Tonight we're going to the movies, and we'll have pizza, and my mom organized our spa day, and—"

"Whoa, Nat! We just got here!" Grace said, laughing. "We haven't even gotten our luggage yet."

Natalie's mom stepped forward and said, "It's nice

to meet you both at last. I've heard so many wonderful things about you. I'll let Noah know you've arrived. He can help us with your suitcases."

"Okay, Mom," Natalie told her.

"Thank you," Alyssa added. She said to Natalie, "Who is Noah?"

"Our driver," Natalie explained.

Grace's eyes widened. "You have a *driver*? Like a chauffeur?" Then she shook her head in wonder. "Of course you do. You're Tad Maxwell's kid!"

"Shhh," Natalie said, putting her finger to her lips. "I'm going incognito. And anyway, it's only sometimes. We asked Noah to drive us because we figured you'd have a lot of luggage."

"Of course we do," Grace said happily. "Oh, girl-friends, we are going to have so much fun!"

"You've got that right!" Natalie cried.

She even believed it herself.

Natalie was sure both Grace and Alyssa had been to the city lots of times, but they ooh'ed and ah'ed at all the bright lights like awestruck first-time tourists as Noah drove the long black town car through Central Park on the way to Natalie's building. Dark-haired Noah was a film major at NYU, working his way through school by driving for the Goodes.

Crossing her high tops at the ankles, Grace said, "Do they have the horse carriages in the winter? It would be fun to get all bundled up and go for a trot around in the snow."

"Oh, I didn't think to put that on the list," Natalie murmured, then smiled as Grace gave her a puzzled look. "I tried to make a list of all the fun things you guys might like to do. Well, a couple of lists, actually. I think they're out here almost all the time, unless it starts snowing again. It's supposed to let up from now until next Monday. I can check and—"

"Chill, Nat!" Grace teased her. "I'm not here to see the city. I'm here to see *you* and the rest of Bunk 3C."

"Same here," Alyssa added. "You know us Jersey girls. We can always pop down here when we're in the mood. A new show on Broadway, a sale at Bloomies . . ."

Grace snapped her fingers. "It's all good!"

Natalie laughed. "Alyssa, never in a million years would you shop at Bloomingdale's. I'll bet you bought that awesome coat in a vintage clothing store."

"I did," Alyssa told her. Her eyes danced. "Salvation Army."

"Get *out*," Natalie said, with even greater admiration.

Seated up front with Noah, Natalie's mom gave her head a quarter-turn, as if to say, *See, Nat? Everything is going to be fine.*

"Hey, do you guys like egg creams?" Natalie asked. "There's a cool new place that serves them."

"Of course! Like Alyssa said, we're East Coast girls!" Grace declared. "What I *really* love is cream soda."

"Oh, good! We bought tons of it," Natalie said. "Lots of diet soda, too. To make sure Alex has a selection."

Alyssa asked, "When are Alex and Brynn showing up?"

"We'll hook up after lunch tomorrow," Natalie said.

"And Jenna's dad is driving her in." She reached out and checked Grace's cute pink watch. She'd worn it at camp last summer. "They're supposed to meet us at our building in about an hour."

"This is going to be so totally awesome!" Grace said happily. "3C, together again."

"Yeah." Natalie nodded. "All of us."

Grace made a little face. "Even Chelsea."

"Now, come on. We promised to be nice," Alyssa reminded Grace. "She's going through a lot. We need to make sure she knows she's part of Bunk 3C through thick and thin."

"Oh, she'll feel the love," Natalie said confidently. "Maybe once she sees how much trouble we've gone to for her, she'll mellow out and be nice to us in return."

"She'll probably take one look at it and decide there's something wrong with it," Grace declared, crossing her arms over her chest.

"*It?* What are you girls talking about?" Natalie's mom asked.

"We have a surprise for Chelsea," Grace told her. "Didn't Natalie tell you about it?"

"It's a surprise, Mom," Natalie said. "A very cool surprise. We've all worked very hard on it."

"Brynn's bringing it," Grace told her. "We're going to give it to her at the all-bunk sleepover. When all of us are there."

"It'll be hard to wait that long," her mother said.

"Yeah, for us, too," Natalie said, and the three girls giggled.

Secrets were fun!

"That's Jenna's *trunk?*" Natalie asked Mr. Bartok as she, Alyssa, and Grace trooped into the lobby. Her mother had remained outside to supervise the unpacking of the luggage.

"Yes, most precious girl," Mr. Bartok replied, his thick white moustache bobbing up and down on his upper lip like a baited hook. "A trunk."

Mr. Bartok was one of their doormen, and had worked in their building since before Natalie was born. He was from Hungary, and he had a very thick Eastern European accent. He usually called Natalie "Natalya" or "most precious girl."

He was standing beside an enormous brown leather trunk that was tipped up on one side. It reminded Natalie of the steamer trunks in the museum dedicated to the early immigrants to America, which was located on Ellis Island. People had traveled with such trunks from their homes in the old country, seeking a new life in America. But back then, they contained all their belongings, not the things they needed for a weekend at a friend's apartment!

A white card taped to the upper left corner of the trunk read "*Jenna Bloom.*" There was a bumper sticker underneath it advertising the Spam Museum in Austin, Minnesota. A tag on the trunk said, "*Jenna Bloom's Trunk Please Take to Natalie Goode's Apt.*"

"But who left it here?" Natalie asked.

"Is note," Mr. Bartok said, handing a small white envelope to Natalie. Natalie opened it and read aloud just as her mother walked up with the driver, who was pushing a luggage cart with Alyssa and Grace's two suitcases and two sleeping bags on it. Mr. Bartok took possession of the cart and Noah walked back through the foyer toward the main entrance.

Hey, Natalie,

I'm Matt, Jenna's science nerd brother. My dad and Jenna will be in NYC soon. I drove separately into the city for a physics seminar at NYU and I offered to bring her trunk to the reunion for her because, as you can see, it's very large. There was no room in my dad's car to stow it.

Have a fun weekend! Don't let Jenzilla take over New York!

Matt Bloom

"Jenzilla. He's the brother who sent her all those wacky bumper stickers," Alyssa said, reading the note over Natalie's shoulder. "He has her same goofy sense of humor."

"There's probably something goofy in here," Natalie guessed. "Like Jenna's own private collection of bowling balls or something."

"Just as long as it's not something dangerous," her mother said. She tested the locks. "Hmm, I can't get it open."

"You want I should find screwdriver?" Mr. Bartok suggested. "Or locksmith?"

"We can probably manage," Natalie's mother said, examining the trunk. "There are wheels set into the base. We can just roll it into the elevator and take it on into our apartment."

"I'm not thinking is good idea," Mr. Bartok announced.

"It'll be all right," Natalie assured him and her mother. They looked dubious. She was a little dubious, herself. Jenna had pulled some awfully wild pranks in her day.

"Okay. Then let's take it on up," Natalie's mother decided.

Mr. Bartok began to push it, gesturing for the others to precede him. "Please to go in, ladies."

Natalie, Grace, Alyssa, and Natalie's mother walked into the elegant mirror elevator. There was plenty of room for the trunk and the luggage cart.

Mr. Bartok hesitated, then carefully guided the trunk over the threshold. The large piece of luggage rattled as it rolled over the narrow gap in the floor.

"I will come with you," he said.

"We can handle it, Mr. Bartok," Natalie's mother assured him.

He hesitated, grunted, and stepped reluctantly back out of the elevator. He anxiously pulled on his moustache as the door closed. Then Natalie's mom keyed in the code to their restricted floor, and the elevator whooshed upward.

"Jenna's up to something," Grace whispered to Natalie. "There's probably a bunch of live animals in this thing. And when you open it, they're going to go crazy all over your apartment."

Natalie's mom looked worried and said, "Nat, do you think that's true?" Grace jerked and made a little uh-oh face, and Natalie guessed that Grace had thought her mom couldn't hear her.

"No way. Jenna learned her lesson at the social." She blanched, realizing she had never told her mother that story. "It'll be okay," she quickly added.

The elevator stopped at the penthouse level and the doors opened. Natalie and her mother wheeled the trunk toward Natalie's front door while Alyssa and Grace pushed the luggage cart.

Just then, Mrs. Goldberg, who lived across the hall, opened her own front door and peered out. She wore a lot of makeup and her white hair was gelled into spikes that stuck straight up.

"Oh, it's you," she said pleasantly. "Hello, girls."

"Hi, Mrs. Goldberg. These are my friends," Natalie said. "The ones who are spending the weekend. Well, the first batch, anyway."

"Hey, we are not cookies," Grace intoned, and the others grinned.

Mrs. Goldberg studied the trunk and the luggage cart. "That's a lot of clothes for a weekend. They must be fashion models."

Grace and Alyssa hid their giggles.

Natalie's mother said, "Mrs. Goldberg is the neighbor who'll be available in case you have an emergency." Natalie's mother was going out later. She and Natalie had permission from the other girls' parents for them to stay in the apartment while she was gone, as long as they promised to check in with Mrs. Goldberg if there were any problems.

"It's nice to meet you," Alyssa said.

Natalie's mom unlocked their front door and pushed it open. Then she pulled on the trunk as Natalie pushed on the other side.

What on earth is Jenna up to? Natalie wondered.

Once the door was shut behind the group, she had her answer. Something began to scratch around inside the trunk. Alyssa covered her mouth and took a step back. Natalie joined her, while Grace rapped on the side of the trunk.

"What's in here?" she demanded. "Hello?"

"I think you girls better stand back while I call 911," Natalie's mother said, and turned to go to the phone in the kitchen.

"Mom, no!" Natalie cried anxiously.

"It might be a crazed lunatic from an insane asylum," her mother said, wringing her hands. "We can't be sure."

"No way," Natalie said. Then, "You think?"

But before Natalie's mother could reply, the trunk popped open!

Jenna herself jumped out!

Her trademark blue Bloom eyes danced as she cried, "Surprise!"

"Jenna Bloom! You maniac!" Natalie shrieked as she threw her arms around her nutty friend. The others hugged her too, laughing at her amazing prank.

Then Jenna turned to Natalie's mother and high-fived her!

"Good job, Ms. Goode!" she said.

"Thanks." Natalie's mom grinned at the three astonished girls.

"You were in on this?" Natalie asked, amazed.

"Natalie, do you *really* think I would bring a strange, person-sized trunk into our house unless I was reasonably sure what was inside it?" her mother asked, giving her one of those mom-looks.

"I guess not," Natalie said; then as her mother raised her brows, she added, "I mean, no way! No way would you do that! And me, neither." She thought a minute. "Did Mr. Bartok know, too?"

"Of course. I called him from the car. It was our prearranged signal."

"Mr. Bartok watched for you. And then I climbed into the trunk right before you guys drove up," Jenna explained.

"You are *evil*," Natalie teased her mom. Wow, her mom was so cool!

"*I* knew it was Jenna," Grace announced. "I was just playing along."

"Oh, *right*." Alyssa elbowed her in the side. "You were freaking out!"

"I was not!" Grace insisted.

"Girls, girls," Natalie's mother said. As they quieted, she looked at Natalie. "Why don't you show the girls around? I'm going to check my messages and then we'll get everyone settled."

"This way, please," Natalie said with a sweep of her arm. "The grand tour will begin!"

Grace, Alyssa, and Jenna followed her into the large living room, which was filled with graceful wood antiques and vases filled with flowers. The drapes were open, revealing the dazzling brilliance of New York City at night.

Hundreds—thousands—of lights twinkled in thousands of windows. Some of the skyscrapers were decorated with elaborate bands of neon, or banks of colored floodlights.

"Oh my gosh," Grace murmured. "Natalie, it looks like a fairyland."

"Very magical," Alyssa agreed. "I want to paint this. I'll use silver paint and lots of jewel tones."

"Come and see the rest," Natalie urged them.

She took them past the guest bathroom and padded

down the hall. The walls were papered in a delicate red overlaid with splashes of gold, very elegant and dramatic.

The first door on the right was her room. Taking a deep breath, she opened it and escorted them in. What would they think?

"Natalie, *wow*," Grace said breathlessly.

Natalie's lacy canopy bed stood against the far wall. Her white antique dresser and desk formed a U, and her computer and printer took up most of the surface of the desk. A bulletin board crisscrossed with dark blue ribbons held tons of photographs, including at least a dozen from camp. There were shots of her bunkmates, and one of her and Simon.

"Hey, *I* took most of these," Jenna said, gazing at them.

"They're really good," Alyssa told her, peering at them. "Nice composition."

Jenna blushed. "Thank you."

"Wow, here's your dad," Grace said, pointing at a row of publicity stills, and then more natural poses of her dad, Natalie, Josie, and a lot of megafamous celebrities. There were movie stars and singers, fashion models and film producers.

"Natalie," Alyssa said slowly, "that's Johnny Depp!"

"Yes." Natalie grinned at her friend. "And he's totally hotter in real life than on the screen."

"Oh my God, *you've met him?*" Jenna stared at Natalie as if she had announced that she was from another planet.

Natalie licked her lips. "Yes, I have."

"Tell us all!" Grace ordered her.

"He's . . . he's really a nice person," she said. *Oh, how lame.*

All eyes remained fixed on her. The butterflies in her stomach began to seriously flutter. Her thoughts jumped to her lists. Now, more than ever, her friends would expect a girl in her position—with serious money and celebrity connections—to pull off an amazing night for them.

I'm still just me, she wanted to tell them. Her throat grew tight and she tried to swallow. But she couldn't. She actually felt a little dizzy.

Just then her mom swept in with a portable phone in her hand. "Shall I go ahead and order the pizzas?" she asked. "You girls must be really hungry."

"Starving," Grace informed her.

Alyssa said, "I hope you don't mind, Ms. Goode, but I'm a vegetarian."

"Already taken into account," Natalie warmly informed her. "Does anyone here like anchovies?"

"Oh, I love them!" Jenna cried. "No one—and I mean absolutely no one—in my family will touch them. Having anchovies on my pizza is a dream come true."

"Good thing you thought to ask, Nat," Natalie's mother said.

Natalie beamed. She said, "We thought we'd get three extra large. One all veggie, of course." She smiled at Alyssa. "And what else shall we get?"

"Anchovies and black olives, definitely," Jenna said.

"Canadian bacon and ham?" Grace asked, checking with the others.

"Works for me," Jenna told her.

"That sounds like three winning combinations," Natalie said. "We'll have lots of leftovers."

"I like cold pizza for breakfast," Alyssa said.

"Me, too," Grace said eagerly. "There's really nothing like it."

"We bought some fresh bagels and croissants," Natalie told them.

"Okay, there *is* something like it," Grace amended, and everyone laughed.

They ordered the pizzas and lounged in the living room by the fireplace while they waited for them, discussing what movie to see. Grace was really excited about *Aces and Kings*, and it was opening night. So the others agreed that they'd go to that.

Then their intercom sounded. Natalie pressed a button in the console beside the fireplace.

"Yes, Mr. Bartok?" she asked.

"Is Miss Hannah," he said.

"Oh, send her on up!" Natalie cried. She smiled at the others. "You'll love Hannah." She nodded at Alyssa. "She's artistic, like you."

"Oh." Alyssa looked less than thrilled. Natalie remembered that Alyssa's parents had sent her to camp to help her become more social. Not that Alyssa didn't know how to make friends. She was just quiet. But maybe Alyssa hadn't counted on meeting anybody new this weekend.

Soon there was a rap on the front door. Natalie called to her mother, "It's Hannah! I'll get it!" She trotted out of the living room, leaving the others behind.

Natalie bounded to the front door and threw it open. Hannah stood on the other side, very cute in a ruffled denim skirt with patchwork on it and a matching light-blue blouse. She wore blue and silver beads in her cornrows, and blue and silver dangly earrings.

Hannah looked really excited. "Did you get my phone message?" she asked as she came into the apartment. "About the award?"

Natalie blinked. "I haven't had a chance to check our voicemail yet. What's up?"

"We each got a call about your portrait of me," Hannah explained. "They judged the art show this afternoon and your sketch got a special jury award! And Helena Attebury, the editor of the school paper, is going to be at the opening tonight and she wants to interview us both!"

Natalie was thrilled. Then she blanched. She had already set up going to Grace's special movie.

"Oh. Oh . . . that's um . . ." She looked anxiously at Grace as she joined Natalie and Hannah in the entryway. She was trying to follow what Hannah was talking about.

Hannah added, "I figured you had something else planned with these guys, but I knew you wouldn't want to skip the art show opening once you knew about the award."

"Your stuff's in an art show?" Grace asked, looking almost as impressed as when Natalie had admitted that she had met Johnny Depp. "That's awesome!"

"It's just a little show at school," Natalie said, feeling even more anxious. It was just going to be some speeches, cookies, and punch, while the parents wandered around and looked at their kids' artwork. The pieces themselves would remain on display for the rest of the semester.

Except for the awards. And the newspaper interview. They were tonight only.

"At your *school*? We can see your school?" Grace was practically bouncing on her toes with eagerness.

"Unless we're not allowed," Jenna added, joining the trio in the foyer. Walking up to Hannah, she stuck out her hand. "Hi. I'm Jenna. One of Natalie's bunkmates."

"It's nice to meet you," Hannah said, shaking hands, but her voice was a little flat. It sounded the way it did when she was being polite around people she didn't especially care to be around.

Jenna turned back to the living room. "Alyssa," she called. "Put down the movie section! Change of plans!"

Then Alyssa walked in. Warmed by the roaring fire, she had taken off the black sweater she had been wearing. She was down to one of her cool black T-shirts. It had only a few paint splatters. Hannah's gaze ticked down to it, then back up to Alyssa's face.

Hannah said, "You must be Alyssa."

"And you're Hannah," Alyssa replied, also a little cool. "Hi."

"So, we're going to an art opening at Natalie's school," Jenna said.

Natalie hesitated. "Except Grace wanted to see that movie . . ." She trailed off. She didn't know what to do.

"If we go to a movie, all we'll do is sit in the dark," Jenna argued. "We could yak and hang out at the art show."

"I was thinking that same thing about the movies,

actually," Grace confessed. "That we wouldn't really get much chance to talk in a movie." She raised her brows as she smiled hopefully at Natalie. "Can we get into the art show? Can you bring guests?"

Natalie felt totally put on the spot. She had assumed her friends wouldn't enjoy wandering around a bunch of sketches, paintings, and sculptures made by other kids. That was why she had planned to skip the show.

Just then, Natalie's mother came out of her office and walked into the foyer. She said, "Good evening, Hannah. Don't you look beautiful!"

Hannah inclined her head. "Thank you, Ms. Goode."

"I just played back our messages," Natalie's mom told Natalie. Her eyes were shining. "Did Hannah tell you about the special jury award? That's so exciting!"

"I think it would be cool to go," Grace interjected. "I'd love to see Natalie's school."

"Oh, her school is in a beautiful old building," her mother said. "Very Art Deco."

Alyssa perked up at the words "Art Deco," and Natalie knew then and there that *all* her friends would rather go to her art show than a movie. She wanted to make sure they had a good time, but it was . . . different from what she'd planned. She really didn't know if they would think it was all that cool once they got there.

"Our school is beautiful," Hannah said, and again, she sounded almost rude.

"I'm sure it is," Alyssa replied.

They sure aren't hitting it off, Natalie thought unhappily.

"Nat, you have tons of cool DVDs," Alyssa said. "I'm sure we'll find at least *three* movies we want to watch when we get back!"

Alyssa was right about that. Natalie's DVD collection was amazing. She was grateful to her friend for pointing out that they could go to the art show and see movies. It looked like another winning combination.

"Okay," Natalie said. "The art show it is."

"Cool!" Grace and Jenna chorused, beaming at her.

"If you're sure," Alyssa said, showing her support for Natalie.

"I'm sure," Natalie said decisively.

Yes, sure—sure that the sleepover wasn't going the way she had planned it. Well, her mom had suggested she leave room for surprises. But she just didn't want there to be any *mistakes*.

chapter
FIVE

"We're free!" Brynn cried as they finished waving at Brynn's mom and shut the front door. "Get ready to rumble!"

"I'm ready!" Alex said as she and Brynn burst into giggles and raced into Alex's room. Alex felt as if the sleepover had officially begun, and she was beyond excited.

As they both dropped onto Alex's bed, Brynn gazed around again with her green eyes at the dozens of trophies, certificates, and ribbons lining Alex's shelves.

"I can*not* get over how many awards you have," Brynn announced. "All you need to complete your collection is Olympic gold."

Alex fondly shook her head as she pushed off her house slippers with her toes and planted her stockinged feet on her turquoise-and-lime green bedspread. "Not even. And I'm not sure the Olympics are in my future."

Brynn sat up and unlaced her tennis shoes. She slid a gaze at her friend and said, "Because of your diabetes?"

Alex wiggled her toes. "I don't know. Maybe. I was this big star in elementary school, but there are a lot of talented players at my middle school. I was kind of on probation on my new team. And at my game last weekend, I totally messed up."

Brynn rested her hand on one elbow as she lay back down beside Alex. Her dark red hair contrasted with the bedspread. "Well, I'll be there to cheer you on tomorrow morning. It's hard to imagine anyone being better than you at any sport!"

Brynn's compliment made Alex feel warm all over. "That's nice of you to say, but it's totally not true. There's so much competition."

Brynn exhaled. "There's so much competition being an actress! *Everyone's* going after the same parts. Being surrounded by dozens of girls you think are prettier than you, and more talented . . . and then being told, 'Sorry, you're just not what we're looking for.'" She grimaced. "It's like being on the team but never getting picked to play."

"Believe me, that stinks the worst," Alex told her. She was so surprised by her own words that she clapped her hand over her mouth.

Brynn laughed. "It does, doesn't it? But I'm willing to go through it for my art."

Alex waved a hand at the rows of glittery trophies. "And then you'll have Oscars and Emmy awards lining the shelves of your fancy Hollywood mansion."

Brynn's eyes took on a faraway look. "That would be nice," she said softly, "but those are the extras. I just want to become the best actress I can be."

Alex thought about that for a minute. "It's hard to

separate winning from playing," she said. "I guess I figure that if I play well, we'll win."

"Only if the others play well, too, if you're on a team," Brynn pointed out. "I know there are MVPs and all, but if you're part of a team, well, you're part of a team."

"Like our bunk," Alex ventured.

"Like our bunk," Brynn agreed. She said, "Speaking of which, did you get the rest of the stuff for Chelsea's present?"

Alex nodded. "It's going to be so cool."

"Great. We can work on it tonight." Brynn scooted off the bed. "So, what's on the evening's agenda?"

Alex got up, too. She said uneasily, "You do remember I have to go to bed pretty early?" She made a face. "Really early, to be honest."

"That's okay," Brynn assured her. "I don't care. It's so fun to be here with you!"

I hope that's true, Alex thought anxiously.

▲ ▲ ▲

She kept hoping it was true. First, Brynn unpacked. Next she and Alex began to discuss what Alex should wear to the reunion, because Alex still wasn't sure about her choice.

Moving to her closet, she showed Brynn her first-choice reunion outfit—her navy polo top, khaki pants, and red accessories. She said, "I'm not sure these really go together. They're from when we were going with my Color War theme."

"Oh, I'm going with the purple, myself," Brynn said. "Aren't you?"

"I don't have anything purple," Alex said in a tight voice. "I look horrible in purple."

"You sound like you're not into our decorating scheme," Brynn ventured.

"I'm not," Alex confessed. "I think it would have been cool if both 3A and 3C did Color War. It would remind everyone that we're rivals."

Brynn nodded eagerly. "I hadn't thought of that. That's true. That would have been totally cool. Wow, I'm really sorry we changed it now."

"I didn't even have a chance to bring it up," Alex said. She frowned. "Once Natalie said it was dumb and purple was better, Julie gave her approval and that was that."

"That stinks," Brynn said hotly.

Alex was grateful for her support. She had felt completely ignored by the entire bunk, plus Julie. Alex was the long-term alumna who had been going to Camp Lakeview forever, not Natalie. Alex was the camper who was always helping the counselors, and doing extra things for the camp . . . and now it was like Natalie was the star of it all. It hurt. A lot.

"Well, there's not much we can do about it now," Alex said, sighing.

"But they should have at least *listened* to you," Brynn argued, putting her hands on her hips. "Natalie just snapped her fingers and everything was the way she wanted it."

"Is that how you really see it?" Alex asked her.

Brynn was totally indignant. "Now that I've had a chance to think about it, yeah. I'm even sorry I'm wearing purple."

Alex pursed her lips tightly together. Now she felt even angrier about the situation.

"Well, there's nothing we can do about it now," she said. "Let's not wreck our overnight."

"Okay. Hey, what do you want to do after dinner?" Brynn asked her, helpfully changing the subject. "We can finish Chelsea's surprise and then maybe watch a movie! Do you like to tell ghost stories? I went to a sleepover where we told each other the scariest stories until, like, three in the morning!"

"Um, don't forget, I have to go to bed early," Alex reminded her again. Butterflies fluttered in her stomach. "I won't have time to do very much after dinner, to be honest."

"Oh." Brynn looked a little shocked. But she quickly covered her dismay with a quick smile. "No problem. I'm a little tired after the drive over here." She grinned at her friend. "We should both rest up so we can enjoy the party and the all-bunk sleepover!"

Alex smiled and nodded, but she wondered again if Brynn was sorry she'd come to Alex's house. She didn't seem sorry, but Brynn was a great actress.

I wish I was half as good a soccer player, Alex thought wistfully. *And I hope I can sleep tonight. I need to rest. But I'm totally amped.*

▲ ▲ ▲

Natalie, Grace, Jenna, Alyssa, Hannah, and Natalie's mom all piled into Hannah's limo to go to the art show. Jenna and Grace were thrilled to be in a real limousine, especially when Hannah invited them to help themselves to the sodas and vast array of snacks. Alyssa didn't drink anything. She sat quietly next to the tinted window, and she seemed mad or something. She didn't even look over when Grace and Jenna started playing video games and turned on the TV.

Natalie was sad that Alyssa and Hannah, her two best friends, didn't seem to like each other. Hannah kept talking about people Alyssa didn't know—like the other kids they hung out with at school. Alyssa just sat there in silence, as if she was counting the minutes until she could get out of the limo.

After a short drive through the busy New York streets, the limo pulled to the curb. The driver opened the door. Then everyone dashed out of the cold air into Natalie's school.

After they checked their coats in the cloakroom, Natalie and Hannah led the way to the room where the art show was being held. There were rows of pegboards hung with pictures. Wooden pedestals held statues and ceramics some of the other students had created.

"Natalie, your picture of Hannah is awesome!" Grace said as the four bunkmates paused in front of Natalie's sketch.

"It's almost scary," Jenna said, pretending to shiver and shake. "It looks so real!"

"It really is beautiful, honey," Natalie's mom agreed.

Alyssa whispered in her ear, "Seriously good work, Nat. And see? Everyone's having a good time."

It was three-quarters true; Jenna, Grace, and Hannah were getting along great. Hannah was cracking up at Jenna's imitation of a statue of a ballet dancer standing on one foot with her arms stretched over her head.

Then Hannah turned her head in Natalie and Alyssa's direction, and she stopped laughing. Alyssa didn't see her, but Natalie did.

Is Hannah jealous of these guys? Natalie wondered. *They're only here for two nights, and then I might not ever see some of them ever again, unless I go to camp. But she and I have all school year to hang out.*

But there was no time to wonder about it; they left soon after that to return home so they would have time to watch movies. Natalie's mom took a cab from the school to her function, after phoning Mrs. Goldberg to let her know the girls were on their way back to the apartment.

Hannah dropped them at the curb, saying good night to everybody . . . except Alyssa. Alyssa didn't seem to notice.

"Thanks again for the lift!" Grace said. "It was awesome."

Mr. Bartok was still on duty, and he had kept their pizzas warm in one of those padded red bags the pizza companies used. Natalie cradled the thick red bag in her arms, announcing, "Three large pizzas weigh a ton!"

Laughing, they clambered into the elevator and went up to Natalie's apartment.

"Let's see if we can IM Alex and Brynn and see what they're up to," Grace suggested. "They said they'd go online tonight to say hi."

"I brought my laptop," Jenna announced.

"I'll help you get everything ready," Alyssa told Natalie.

"I'll help Jenna," Grace announced.

Natalie and Alyssa went together into the kitchen. Natalie set the plates on the counter and got out some napkins. Alyssa opened the three pizza boxes and said, "There's enough pizza here for the whole bunk!"

"I guess I got carried away," Natalie confessed. "I didn't want anyone to go hungry."

"No worries. We'll be stuffing ourselves silly," Alyssa told her. She put double slices on each white plate.

"We've got them!" Jenna cried. "Alex and Brynn are online!"

Alyssa and Natalie each picked up two plates and carried them into the living room. Jenna had her laptop on her lap, and Grace was leaning sideways, staring at the screen.

"Ooh! They're in their pajamas, and they've . . . eaten dinner," Grace said slowly. "That's *it*?"

"Maybe she got there late," Alyssa said.

"We haven't even eaten dinner," Jenna pointed out. "I'll tell them they're ahead of us!" She typed in her message.

Natalie said, "What does everyone want to drink?"

Everyone gave her their requests. As Alyssa moved to help her, Natalie shook her head and said, "Take a load off, Lyss. I can get them."

"Type, 'We're in Nat's city!'" Grace said to Jenna as Jenna's hands hovered over the laptop keyboard. "Tell them about the art show!"

"Yeah, be sure to tell them how much fun you're having," Natalie teased.

Aries8: We're having 2 much fun! We went to an art show at Nat's school in Hannah's limo!

In Alex's room, Alex's heart started beating a little too fast as she read Jenna's IM over Brynn's shoulder. Brynn was seated at Alex's computer desk, in charge of typing their replies.

Alex had no doubt they were doing all kinds of exciting things at Natalie's sleepover. Maybe Natalie had invited some movie stars over. Or her dad was there. All far more thrilling than sitting around in Alex's room talking about going to bed early!

Aries8: We're eating so much pizza we won't be able to fit into our kewl outfits! Wah!

BrynnWins: New York pizza's the best in the universe! My fave is black olives and shrooms. My mouth is watering!

Grrrrace: You guys are lucky. You'll get some exercise. But tomorrow we have to lie around in a spa! Tough luck, right?

"That sounds so cool," Brynn said to Alex. "Have you ever had a facial? I'm going to have one for my next birthday."

"No, I have never had a facial," Alex said unhappily. But she wasn't sure Brynn even heard her. It was obvious Brynn was amped over Natalie's sleepover. Alex should have realized her boring old life could never compete with Natalie's exciting New York adventures.

NatalieNYC: hi! nat here! my mom just donated some kewl purple zebra print napkins and sunglasses for our table.

"I almost forgot about the purple problem," Brynn said to Alex.

But Alex was even madder. She sputtered, "I *asked* if there was anything I could get at the party store when I went to return my blue and red napkins and the table-cloth. And Julie said no!"

"I guess she thought Natalie's napkins were more 'trendy,'" Brynn said, making air quotes. "Natalie really is rubbing it in."

NatalieNYC: u **SO** should have come down 2nite! when u guys come in tomorrow we'll have lunch & decorate our table. Julie sez we can go in 30 min early.

Alex was humiliated. *She* was the one who got to do stuff like that, not Natalie Goode! It was like the whole reunion had become Natalie's personal property. Even though this had been her first summer at Camp Lakeview, and Alex was a mega-legacy, everyone was letting Natalie run it. Just because she was rich and her father was an international movie star and she lived in New York. It wasn't fair!

"Scoot over," she said to Brynn. Brynn rose out of Alex's desk chair and Alex sat down.

SoccerLover: Well, I hope you & YOUR friends have fun at YOUR reunion!

Alex logged off.

There was a moment of silence in Alex's bedroom as her computer powered down. Then Brynn said, "Whoa."

"I'm sorry," Alex said. She was trembling. "I just lost it."

"No, Natalie really dissed you," Brynn added. "Just completely ignoring all your hard work to get things for the table. I'm proud of you for sticking up for yourself."

Alex gazed up at her. Brynn nodded at her. "You've got what my mom calls moxie."

"Moxie?" In spite of her freakout, Alex laughed. "It sounds like a disease!" Her voice dropped. "Do you really think I should have said that?"

"Yeah! Natalie was just lording it over us how much more fun they're having than us," Brynn said. Then her eyes got huge, as she realized what she'd just said. "Oh, Alex, I didn't mean it that way!"

Alex felt even worse. But she forced herself to smile as she said, "I know. It's okay."

A wave of dizziness overcame her and she added, "I'm sorry, Brynn, but I have to go to bed now. I know it's early, but I'm worn out. It happens."

"Oh, I'm totally fine with that," Brynn assured her. "But I don't know if I can sleep. I'm so irritated with those guys!"

Alex knew how she felt. But she also knew how she would feel in the morning if she didn't get enough rest. So she resolutely went through her nightly ritual— brushing her teeth, washing her face, and climbing into her bed.

Brynn slithered into her sleeping bag on the floor

beside her and said, "Good night! Don't let the bedbugs bite!"

"I won't," Alex said feebly.

Then Alex turned out the light and stared into the darkness for what seemed like forever.

▲ ▲ ▲

The next thing she knew, she sleepily opened her eyes and looked at her clock. It was only one in the morning, and she wondered why she had awakened.

She whispered, "Brynn?"

There was no answer.

Alex got up and tiptoed out of her room. There was a light on in the living room. Brynn was curled up in her dad's leather recliner with a book. Her head was down, and Alex couldn't tell if she was reading or sleeping.

She said softly, "Brynn?"

Brynn didn't respond. Alex didn't know what to do. If Brynn was asleep, she didn't want to wake her up.

She tiptoed back into her room and climbed back into bed.

I'll go check on her in a little while, she decided, bunching up her pillow. Then she turned out the light. *Some fun for Brynn, reading a book while I snooze. I'm sure she'd rather be at snobby Natalie's.*

Natalie, who's stealing all the fun!

chapter

SIX

Alyssa sat next to Natalie on the couch as the girls devoured microwave popcorn and watched *Dying Too Young* on Natalie's widescreen TV. Natalie had state-of-the-art high-definition *everything*.

"Have Alex or Brynn come back online?" Natalie whispered in her ear.

"No," Alyssa whispered back.

Everyone had gone over the entire IM conversation a million times, but no one had a clue why Alex had gotten so mad at Natalie. Alyssa suggested they phone, but Natalie said no. Alex had logged off, and that meant she wanted her space.

"This movie is depressing me," Grace groaned. "It's about people dying!"

It *was* very depressing. The lead character was a young mother who had just had a baby and then discovered she had an incurable disease.

"Hello? Title? *Dying Too Young?*" Jenna said impatiently. "You voted to watch it."

"Well, only because I've already seen the *Super Ninja Twins* like sixty times!" Grace insisted. That had been Jenna's choice.

It was as if Natalie's bad mood had infected everyone like a virus.

"Well, I'm glad Chelsea's not here to see it," Alyssa said softly. "A movie about dying would not be cool for her."

"You're right," Natalie replied. At the mention of Chelsea, she got nervous all over again.

"Shhh, the doctor's coming in with her test results," Grace said, the silhouette of her hand gesturing at the screen. "Maybe it's good news."

"I hope so. The doctor is a total hottie," Jenna said. "So maybe they'll get married or something."

Natalie murmured to Alyssa, "I thought I would have the most problems getting along with Chelsea. Now I'm dreading seeing Alex."

"It'll be okay," Alyssa counseled her best friend. She patted her arm. "You'll see."

"Oh, no!" Grace cried in the darkness. "Natalie, I just dropped my pizza sauce-side-down all over your mom's carpet!"

Natalie winced as she leaped to her feet. She said, "Blot it with the napkins. I'll get the cleaning stuff. Don't feel bad, Grace. It happens all the time."

But the truth was . . . it didn't. Natalie's local friends were supercareful when they came over.

"I'll help you," Alyssa told her.

"Thanks," Natalie replied gratefully.

They dashed into the kitchen together.

"More napkins!" Grace yelled.

As Natalie grabbed a roll of paper towels and a spray bottle of stain remover, she glanced at the clock on the microwave. It was after one in the morning. Her mom was in bed, sleeping through everything. That was where Natalie wished *she* were. Her nerves were frayed. Alex was mad at her, Hannah might be mad at her, and her friends were trashing her apartment! She wanted to turn off the movie and tell everyone to go to bed.

Then they'll all be mad at me, she thought.

"Grace!" she heard Jenna moan. "You used up all the napkins!"

"Well, there's tons of gooey cheese and ham, okay?" Grace replied.

As Natalie headed back toward the living room, she teared up, overwhelmed. It was only the first night of the big weekend, and she had had it.

"Hey, we'll get it cleaned up, okay?" Alyssa said, giving Natalie's arm a squeeze. "Tomorrow morning, no one will even be able to tell there was a mess."

"Thanks," Natalie said, meaning it. But tomorrow morning seemed very, very far away.

🔺 🔺 🔺

Alex woke on Saturday morning with a start. Her clock radio blared a way-too-perky pop song as she groaned and fumbled for the snooze button. Then she stopped herself. Snoozing was not an option. She had to get up and get going if she was going to make her soccer game on time.

It was still dark in her room. She flicked on the lamp and peered into the darkness. Brynn was asleep in her sleeping bag, with one arm thrown over her head. Alex wondered how late Brynn had remained in the living room.

She got up and tiptoed over to Brynn, gazing down at her by the soft light of the lamp.

"Brynn?" she whispered. "We have to get up for my soccer game, okay?"

Brynn didn't move.

"Brynn?" she whispered more loudly.

There was still no response.

She touched her sleeping bag and gave it a little nudge. Nothing.

Alex didn't know what to do. Brynn had said she wanted to watch Alex's game, but she was so tired, Alex was having trouble waking her up. Brynn would want to be rested for all the fun at the party and Natalie's sleepover.

Alex decided to think about it as she got on her soccer uniform. But after she had dressed in her dark blue shorts and white jersey, pulled her hair into a ponytail, and brushed her teeth, Brynn was still fast asleep.

On her way into the kitchen, Alex spotted a book balanced on the arm of the recliner. She picked it up and examined the title. It said, NEW YORK CITY: 101 COOLEST PLACES TO GO.

She turned to a page that Brynn had marked by folding down the corner. It was labeled THEATER SCENE. In the margin she had written, *Ask Natalie about this!*

There were a lot of other pages turned down at the corners. Brynn had read and studied her guidebook with as much care as Alex would give a textbook. Being rested for their trip to the city was surely more important to Brynn than watching Alex's stupid soccer game.

Alex scrambled some eggs and toasted English muffins. Everything was ready when her mom walked into the kitchen. She was wearing jeans and a sweatshirt that read SOCCER MOM! ASK ME HOW!

Yawning, she said, "Good morning, honey. Ready for your game?" They talked in low voices so they wouldn't wake up Alex's father and brother, who both had the luxury of sleeping late.

"Yes," Alex replied. She dished the scrambled eggs onto two plates.

"What about Brynn?" her mom asked, as she picked up the plates and carried them to the dining room table. "Isn't she joining us?"

"She stayed up really late. I think she'd rather sleep," Alex said, sitting down. She picked up her fork and began to eat the fluffy eggs.

"Oh?" Her mom cocked her head. "At dinner she said she couldn't wait to see you play."

"That was before she stayed up all night reading," Alex confided. "I know she doesn't want to be tired for the reunion."

"Maybe you should ask her what she wants," her mom said.

"Then she'll be awake," Alex pointed out. "Anyway, there's no time now." She gestured with her fork at the clock. "We have to leave as soon as we're finished eating."

Her mom glanced at the clock. "Oh! You're right about that. But I hope she's not too disappointed."

"Trust me, Mom," Alex said. "I know what I'm doing."

Only, she didn't, exactly. She really, really, really hoped she was doing the right thing. But she wasn't totally positive she was.

I hope Brynn's okay with this.

"Hey, sleepyheads," Natalie's mom called to the four girls cocooned in their sleeping bags. "It's time to get up, or you'll miss your spa day."

Natalie slowly raised her head, to see her mom in a pair of black yoga pants and a tight-fitting black workout top. She had probably worked out in her bedroom, something she did when she was too busy to get to the gym.

"Hi, Mom," Natalie said sleepily.

She and the others had rolled out their sleeping bags after *Dying Too Young* (luckily, the cute doctor had saved the mom's life and then they had gotten married). They must have dozed off during their next movie. It was a silly comedy titled *Summer Secrets*, directed by Natalie's dad's friend, Haley Schricker.

"I've got fresh croissants and muffins heated and waiting," her mother said. "And hot chocolate."

"You know how to tempt a kid," Natalie told her. She sat up and yawned. "But I'm still half-asleep!"

Jenna, Grace, and Alyssa were also slowly waking, stretching and murmuring good morning to each other. Although the scene was very different from the post-bugle call rush of their bunk, it reminded Natalie of their mornings at Camp Lakeview. It gave her a comfortable feeling, reminding her that these girls were old friends of hers.

Plus, they had done an awesome job cleaning up the pizza disaster. There was no stain on the thick gray carpet!

"I need to go into the gallery for a while," Natalie's

mom told her. "I'll take you to the spa on my way, but you're going to have to hurry to make it on time. Then you guys can relax and enjoy all your beauty treatments."

It was a lucky thing there were three full bathrooms in the apartment—one in Natalie's mom's suite; one in Natalie's room; and the guest bathroom. Since Natalie's mom had to get ready for her day, too, that left two bathrooms for four girls. What a luxury compared to the single bathroom at camp!

But everyone seemed to be out of practice with hurrying. Despite her efforts to be patient, Natalie was almost pacing by the time it was her turn to take a shower. Then after that, she had to blow-dry her hair and do her makeup.

All four of them devoured the buttery, flaky croissants and muffins loaded with blueberries and walnuts. No one ate the cold pizza. Natalie drank down her sweet, warm hot chocolate in four gulps.

As they finished up and carried their plates into the kitchen, Natalie relaxed a little. Even if they were a teeny bit late, the next three hours were fully planned. Everyone was sure to have fun at an exclusive New York spa!

They took the car to the spa. Natalie's mom accompanied them. As Noah pulled the car over, Natalie's mom called Skye, the spa receptionist, on her cell phone.

"Okay, they're on their way," she told Skye. She hung up and gave Natalie a kiss as the girls piled out of the car.

They went inside the building and into a brass elevator.

"Take a last look at the old us!" Grace said as she stuck out her tongue at herself in the reflective surface.

They zoomed to one of the highest floors, and the elevator opened. Ahead stood the frosted glass double door of the spa.

Natalie led the way. Skye greeted them, rising from behind her oval glass desk. She was wearing a white gauze tunic and flowing jade green skirt. Her hair was gathered back in a sloppy bun and she wore hardly any makeup. Her skin glowed.

There was a simple stone wall behind her desk. A sheet of water flowed gently over it. Soft flute music played softly in the background.

"It's so nice to see you, Natalie," she said, as Natalie introduced each of her friends. "Welcome to our spa."

She handed each girl a little booklet outlining all the beauty treatments the spa provided. Natalie had seen it before, of course, and she had already planned out what she was going to have: a manicure, a pedicure, and a facial.

"Oh," Jenna said slowly, turning the pages. "There sure is a lot to pick from."

"I'll say," Grace agreed, scratching her head. She looked at Skye. "What do you recommend?"

"Well, it depends on what you'd like to get out of your session. Some of our clients come to relax. Others come to have makeup applied, or to get a haircut."

One of the spa employees, a young woman with short, spiky hair, appeared from behind the stone wall with a flat stone-colored tray. There were four handleless cups and a plate of flat orange discs.

"Please refresh yourselves with some herbal tea and dried mango," Skye invited them.

"Dried mango?" Grace asked, looking hesitant.

"Thank you." Alyssa took a cup of tea and a piece of mango. She bit into the mango. "Oh, this is great," she enthused.

Jenna and Grace picked up teacups and pieces of mango. Natalie took the last teacup. She glanced up at the clock. Because they were late, they were already almost fifteen minutes into their three-hour booking. She started to feel nervous.

"You guys, you need to decide what you're going to have done," she said.

"Okay, okay," Grace said, drinking down her tea.

"What I would recommend for you is a nice spa manicure and a pedicure," Skye told Grace. "And perhaps a hot oil treatment for your hair."

"My hair?" Grace frowned and touched her crazy mass of curls. "Is there something wrong with it?"

"No, of course not," Skye said easily. "It's beautiful. The hot oil treatment is simply to pamper it."

"Oh." Grace exhaled, looking a little happier. "Okay, that sounds fun."

Jenna said, "I'd like to get a French manicure and pedicure. I'd like to get flowers painted on my nails, too."

"Fingers and toes? We can do that. We can use little jewels for the centers of the flowers," Skye told her.

"Cool!" Jenna cried.

"Can I get my hair cut?" Alyssa asked.

"Ah, a brave one," Skye said approvingly. She

cocked her head and studied Alyssa, as if seeing her in a brand-new look.

"Brave? A haircut *is nothing* for this wild child," Jenna scoffed. "You should have seen what she did to her hair last summer."

Everyone giggled at the memory of Alyssa's dye job—instead of the cool red tint she had been aiming for, she had wound up looking like Ronald McDonald. But Alyssa had figured out a way to make that fashion disaster seem cool.

"Well, I'd like a haircut and some acrylic nails," Alyssa said decisively. "And I want the nails to be dark, dark purple."

"Whoa." Grace, Jenna, and Natalie stared at her.

"You do realize," Skye said, "that if you get acrylic nails you'll have to maintain them once you get home?"

Alyssa nodded. "Or take them off, right? With acetone?"

At the stares the others were giving her, Alyssa said, "What? Nat and Marissa spent all summer reading fashion magazines. I *did* listen."

Skye lifted Alyssa's hand and examined her nails. She said, "We could easily paint your own nails dark purple. Perhaps instead of the acrylics, we could add some temporary purple highlights to your hair."

"Purple highlights . . . hmm," Alyssa considered. "Let me think."

Think quickly, Lyss! Natalie glanced again at the clock. Now they were almost *twenty* minutes into their three hours. She tried to signal to Alyssa that she had to make up her mind. But Alyssa was glancing down at the pages of the spa booklet.

"Let's see . . ." Alyssa said.

"Alyssa," Natalie blurted. "Please hurry."

Alyssa glanced at her. "Oh, sorry." She shut the booklet. Her cheeks were pink. "Whatever."

"The haircut, the highlights, and a manicure with purple polish?" Skye asked her.

"Sure." Alyssa smiled, but she didn't look totally okay with the plan.

"You should get what you want," Natalie said, feeling bad for rushing her best friend.

"It's cool. I'll love it," Alyssa told her.

"Okay. Natalie, you're the last one to pick," Skye said. "What would you like?"

"A manicure, a pedicure, and a facial," she said.

"Oh." Skye crinkled her forehead. "I'm not certain we'll have time for all that. But we can try," she said, smiling. "All right?"

I knew it! Natalie thought. She was disappointed. But she reminded herself that she would have plenty of other chances to come to the spa. She smiled politely and said, "All right."

"Okay." Skye gathered their little booklets. The other employee collected their teacups. "If you will all follow me, I'll show you where to put your clothes."

"Put our clothes?" Grace cried. "Are we going to get undressed?"

"Not if you would prefer to stay in your own things," Skye explained. "We provide special robes for you to wear while you're here."

"Oh." Grace looked at the others. "Are you guys going to wear them?"

"I am," Natalie told her.

Alyssa nodded.

"O-kay, then," Grace said, taking a deep breath. "Let's do it!"

chapter
SEVEN

Alex's soccer game was a disaster.

And it was Alex's fault.

She was distracted, and it showed in her play-ing. She was nervous about winning the game for her team—or at least, not losing it for them! The pressure made her try too hard, and she started kicking the ball out of bounds twice in a row. After that she hung back, letting another team member—*any* other team member—take the ball.

She tried to remember her mantra—*I know I can, I know I can*—but she just couldn't keep her mind on the game. Her teammates looked more and more unhappy with her as the other team continually took the ball and scored off her errors.

I wish Brynn were here, she thought. Not to watch how well (or how badly!) Alex played. Right now, she needed a friend who didn't care if she totally messed up. Someone to be supportive of her and not judge her.

Maybe it was the stress of worrying, or maybe she hadn't gotten enough sleep. But by the time the game ended—with a win for the other team—Alex had a pounding headache. She remembered the last time her head had hurt this much. It was at camp, just before she had gone into diabetic shock.

She told her mom about it on the drive home. Her mother gave her a piece of candy to eat and said, "We're going to have a good lunch, and you're going to take a nap."

"But Mom! Brynn and I will miss our bus!" Alex protested.

"And after your nap, we'll discuss whether or not you feel up to going to the reunion," her mom added.

Her stomach flipped. *Not go? To the reunion?*

"But, *Mom!*" she argued. "If *I* can't go, *Brynn* can't go."

"Just take a good nap and we'll see, all right?" her mother said firmly.

Alex nodded glumly and looked out the window.

As soon as they pulled up to the house, Brynn burst out of the front door. She was dressed in her reunion outfit and her hair was curled. And she looked very, very mad.

"I can't believe you!" she cried. She stomped right up to Alex as she got out of the car. "Why didn't you wake me up?"

Alex's mom gave her a sympathetic smile, then walked into the house. The two girls were left alone outside.

"I got up in the middle of the night, Brynn. I saw you reading in the living room," Alex confessed. "I was afraid you'd be too tired to have any fun in New York. So I let you sleep."

Brynn rolled her eyes. "What are you, my mother? You knew I wanted to go to your game! I *asked* you to wake me up!"

"I know." Alex exhaled heavily. "I'm sorry." She touched her temples. "I didn't know what to do and . . ." Her head hurt too much to go into it. "Brynn, I don't feel good. I need to lie down." She closed her eyes and put her hands to her forehead.

"Alex, are you going to faint?" Brynn cried, putting a steadying hand on Alex's shoulder. "Mrs. Kim! Alex needs you!"

"Shhh," Alex pleaded, her head throbbing. "My mom knows. She's the one who told me to lie down." She dropped her hands to her sides and trudged toward the house. "I'm sorry to make you wait to go to New York."

"Don't be dumb," Brynn said. "It's more important that you feel better."

"That's how I felt about waking you up for the game," Alex explained. "It was more important that *you* got enough rest. You *know* what it's going to be like to have an all-bunk sleepover. What if you were just too tired to enjoy it?"

Then she realized she had to tell Brynn what her mother had said. She bit her lower lip.

"Brynn, my mom told me that if I don't feel better, I won't be allowed to go at all."

Brynn's eyes widened. "Oh, no!"

"I know." She nodded. "So I'd better go take that nap, okay?"

"Yes, sure. Oh, Alex!" Brynn gave her a big hug. "Don't worry. Even if we can't go, we'll have fun together."

Alex was nearly in tears. Brynn was, too. She knew Brynn was just trying be a good friend. How much fun had she had so far? And how could *anything* they did compare to missing the reunion?

Alex said, "You are being really cool about the situation. Thank you so much, Brynn."

"It's no biggie," Brynn said, her cheeks reddening. "Go. Rest."

"I will totally rest," Alex promised.

As Alex headed for her bedroom, her mom brought her a sandwich and took a fingerstick to check her blood sugar level. She looked down at the little readout and said, "It's good, honey. Maybe you're just overtired. Have some food and take that nap."

She said to Brynn, "She needs some time alone, all right, Brynn?"

"Okay." Brynn smiled very hard. "Can I help with anything? Do you need some vegetables chopped?"

"No, thank you. Maybe you'd like to watch a movie," Alex's mom said. "I'll show you what we have."

Alex's mom walked with Brynn toward the shelves where they kept their DVDs. Alex took that as her cue to go into her room.

She shut her door as she gobbled down half of the sandwich.

Then she froze, and caught her breath.

Draped over her desk chair was a totally sweet outfit!

Brynn had pulled it together for her, and it was incredible. Brynn had paired Alex's navy blue polo shirt with her black jeans. That would have looked plain and boring, the kind of thing Alex wore. But then Brynn had added a sense of drama by threading a feathery black and silver fringe scarf through the belt loops. The scarf was nothing like anything Alex owned—although she had been wanting a fringed scarf forever. And to use it as a belt was beyond cool.

Then Brynn had arranged a black velvet choker over the neckline of the navy blue top. A silver half moon dangled from the center of the choker. Two black barrettes balanced on either shoulder. They were decorated with silver beads that caught the sparkle of the silver moon.

It was completely, totally *perfect* for the reunion!

She thought about calling out to Brynn to thank her, but she knew she would end up trying on the outfit with her. To get to the reunion she needed to quietly finish her sandwich and get some rest.

Smiling big-time, feeling better already, she walked to her closet and found her black flats. She wished she had some silver ones, but Alex had always been a conservative dresser.

Until today, she thought excitedly. *And I have Brynn to thank for my bold new look!*

Maybe Brynn had been angry with her for leaving her at home, but that hadn't stopped her from being a great best friend.

I've got to feel better, Alex told herself. *No way am I keeping Brynn from going to that reunion!*

▲ ▲ ▲

Natalie was having trouble enjoying her manicure.

Getting her nails buffed, polished, and dried took too long. She was twenty minutes over the three hours her mother had booked with the spa.

She was very hungry. It had been hours since breakfast, and all they had had to eat since then were a few bites of dried mango and a cup of tea.

Skye came in. She said, "Would you like some more tea or water?"

"Um, I'm okay," Natalie said. "Are the others all done?"

"Yes," Skye assured her. "They're fine. They're entertaining themselves in the reception area."

Natalie was afraid to ask what that meant.

Through the closed door she heard a lot of high-pitched laughter. She recognized Grace's giggle and closed her eyes. She said, "I'm sorry about the noise."

"I *will* have to go ask them to be a little quieter," Skye said. "Excuse me."

Finally, her nails were done. She hurried back into her clothes and rushed to the reception area.

Her three friends were sitting in chairs facing her. Alyssa looked fantastic in a stylin' new haircut—but Grace and Jenna were a couple of freaks! Their faces were covered with blue goo and they were holding lime-colored cotton balls over their eyelids.

Natalie burst into shocked giggles. They were imitating the photograph Jenna had snapped of her sister, Stephanie, who had been a CIT in Bunk 3A. They had given the picture to Tyler, the swim instructor, whom Stephanie was crushing on. Stephanie had been furious.

"You guys!" Natalie cried.

"Surprise!" Jenna boomed as she and Grace took the cotton balls off their eyes. Alyssa just smiled quietly and shook her head.

Just then, a man and a woman in black suits and wrap-around sunglasses walked through the frosted glass entrance doors of the spa. Natalie knew them. They were Hannah's mother's security detail. Since she was an ambassador, she occasionally traveled with two bodyguards in tow.

The two bodyguards froze when they saw Natalie's three friends. The man raised his wrist toward his mouth and said, "Delay the ambassador's entrance."

"It's all right!" Natalie assured them. "These are my . . . friends. They're visiting me."

As she spoke, Grace and Jenna sat up straight, like little girls who had been sent to the principal's office.

Skye appeared next. She came from behind the water wall and said, "Oh, the ambassador is here." She stared with dismay at Natalie's two blue-faced friends.

"We'll go wash our faces," Jenna said, getting to her feet. She looked guilty. Natalie figured she was the one who had thought up the prank.

Before they had a chance to make a quick exit, the spa doors opened again. Hannah's exotic mother paused regally at the threshold.

Skye gushed, "Ambassador. How lovely to see you this morning."

"Hello, Skye. And Natalie," Hannah's mother said, embracing Natalie. "What a pleasant surprise. Is your mother here?"

"No, I'm here with my friends," Natalie replied.

Alyssa and Grace both rose—only Grace moved so fast that she knocked over her chair.

"Sorry!" she blurted. Her pink lips were a bizarre contrast to her bright blue face.

Natalie introduced them one by one to Hannah's mother.

Grace did a sort of curtsey. "We're the Blue Girl Group," she explained.

Despite her initial embarrassment, Natalie laughed. Grace was making a reference to the very weird performance group called the Blue Man Group. Natalie had seen them perform, and she had liked them a lot.

"Perhaps you could perform at my embassy sometime," Hannah's mother teased. "We encourage an exchange of cultures."

"We're kind of our own culture," Jenna added.

"Camp Lakeview culture," Grace added.

"Do you know if your mother is free for lunch today?" Hannah's mother asked Natalie. "I've just discovered the most fascinating Ethiopian restaurant. They have the best *engera* I have ever tasted." She leaned toward the girls. "That's a kind of bread."

"I love Ethiopian food," Alyssa offered. "I'm a vegetarian."

Hannah's mother raised her brows. "Then you must try this restaurant. It's called Teff, Natalie. It's across the street from Rockefeller Center. Just a little way past the Hilton."

"Is it *Teff* to get in?" Grace wisecracked. When the ambassador just blinked at her, she added, "I mean, do you need reservations?"

"Not if you're Tad Maxwell's daughter," Hannah's mother replied, her eyes twinkling. "You should take your friends, sweetie. It's just wonderful."

"That's a great idea!" Natalie said, thrilled. A cool new New York restaurant. Her friends would be able to brag about it when they got home.

"Ambassador, we'll be bringing you some tea and mango slices in your private room," Skye said. Just as she spoke, the same spiky-haired young woman appeared with the same stone tray, one teacup, and some familiar-looking orange discs.

"This way, ma'am," the woman said.

The ambassador began to follow her. She said over her shoulder, "Good-bye, Natalie. I'll tell Hannah I saw you."

She disappeared behind the water wall.

"Thanks," Natalie called to her.

"I hope we didn't, like, freak her out," Grace said.

"We look like space aliens!" Jenna wailed. "I was a freak in front of a woman who has her own limo!"

"No way," Natalie said lightly. "After all, this *is* a spa."

"In New York City," Alyssa added.

"Well, let's go wash our faces before someone else Natalie knows shows up," Jenna said. "Like Jesse McCartney or Hayden Christensen or somebody!"

The two scurried away. Alyssa stayed while Natalie went over the gi-normous bill with Skye. It was all good. Her mom had told her how much they could spend and they had stayed well under the limit.

"Do you need us to chip in?" Alyssa asked, sounding anxious.

"No, it's fine," Natalie told her. "It's on my mom."

"That's really generous of her," Alyssa said. "You

know I could *never* afford in a million years to come to a place like this."

"Don't even say that, Lyss," Natalie chided her. "Someday you're going to be a rich and famous artist. *You'll* be the one taking us to fancy places!"

"Yeah, in my private jet," Alyssa drawled, but Natalie could tell she was catching fire a little bit.

"Why not? My dad was dirt-poor when he was our age." Natalie decided to skip over the fact that now he did actually own a private jet.

"Well, it's nice to dream." Alyssa gave Natalie's hand a squeeze. "And to have a friend who has faith in me."

"Of course I do! What are friends for?" Natalie replied.

About a minute later, Jenna and Grace returned with freshly scrubbed faces.

"Oh, I am so totally exfoliated!" Grace quipped, patting her cheeks. "I look younger, right?"

"Yeah, you're ten again!" Jenna said. The two started cracking up.

Skye returned with four mango-colored paper sacks with straw handles. Natalie opened hers to find samples of the spa's line of products—a tiny bar of peach-colored soap, a little bottle of hand lotion, and a vial of body mist. Everyone started opening the bottles and spraying themselves with body mist.

"Mango-scented body spray! Yum!" Grace said, sniffing the air like a rabbit.

Natalie had an idea. "Skye, may I buy some more of these?" She turned to the other girls. "We can put them on our table. We need ten more for the bunk, including Marissa and Julie."

"Cool!" said Grace.

"Is this for the big party you're attending?" Skye asked. "Your mother mentioned it when she booked your spa time."

"Yes," Natalie told her.

"We'd be happy to make a gift of them, then," Skye told her. "It was such a pleasure having all of you here."

Soon the girls were carrying a large spa bag containing the extra gift sacks. As Natalie thanked her again, Skye replied. "We hope you'll come again soon."

Was it Natalie's imagination, or did she sound relieved that they were leaving?

EIGHT

The four girls took the elevator to the street level. The doorman nodded at them as they pushed through the revolving glass door.

Outside, the day had warmed, and the snow was melting. Sunshine glistened on the high-rises. The eight-lane street before the girls was bumper-to-bumper with cars blaring their horns. The sidewalk was almost as crowded, with New Yorkers in their winter coats and caps.

Half-yelling to be heard, Natalie said, "Okay. I'll take you to Teff. Maybe we can meet my mom there." She handed the large sack to Alyssa so she could get her cell phone out of her purse.

"Hey, no offense, but that restaurant sounds weird," Grace said, stopping Natalie by putting her hand on her wrist.

"Yeah, and we're not very dressed up," Jenna put in. "I'd feel funny eating someplace an ambassador eats wearing jeans and a sweater."

Natalie looked to Alyssa. Her best friend moved her shoulders, as if to say, *Hey, whatever you want to do, I'm fine with it.*

"Well . . ." Natalie was stuck.

"Did you already have a plan for lunch?" Alyssa asked her.

"Yes. I have a list of about four places," Natalie began. She opened her purse and rummaged around for the correct pieces of black paper. "Hold on. We got out a little later than I expected, but . . . let's see, where's the list—"

"Hey, look!" Grace interrupted, pointing. "Hot dogs!"

Sure enough, there was a hot dog cart on the corner of their block. A short, wiry man in a black cloth jacket stood behind a large aluminum box on wheels. A colorful red-and-white-striped umbrella shielded him from the sun.

"My mouth is *so* watering," Grace announced. "Let's snag some hot dogs, okay, Nat?"

Jenna bounced on the balls of her toes. "Please, please, please?"

"Alyssa's a vegetarian," Natalie argued. Eating Hebrew Nationals from a cart was definitely not part of the plan! She had three really swanky, famous restaurants on her lunch list, plus the cool new retro place that served egg creams.

"Actually, it says on his sign that he also has tofu hot dogs. I love them," Alyssa said.

"Oh, come on, Natalie," Grace pleaded. "I'm so hungry, I'm about to faint. By the time we go somewhere else and sit down and order, it'll be time to get ready for the reunion."

Jenna nodded hard, clasping her hands and placing them beneath her chin, begging like a sad-eyed kitty cat.

"Grace has a point," Alyssa said, taking their side.

Natalie thought of the hours she had spent on the Internet, Googling restaurant names and studying their menus. How she'd made sure they were open on Saturdays and if they required reservations.

"Fine," she grumbled. "We'll have hot dogs."

She reached for the large sack filled with goody bags. Alyssa said, "It's okay. I'll carry it for a while."

Natalie tried to maintain her composure as she led the way to the vendor. He had a droopy face and a dark moustache. He was wearing a New York Giants baseball cap. Natalie thought of Sarah, who often wore a Boston Red Sox cap. It hit her that she was having trouble entertaining just three of her bunkmates. Tonight she would have ten of them!

"What'll it be, ladies?" the vendor asked pleasantly.

"Get whatever you want," Natalie said curtly. "My mom gave me plenty of money to pay for lunch."

"You don't have to pay for everything all the time," Grace said. "We're not poor, you know."

Natalie's mouth dropped open. Was Grace dissing her? She couldn't believe it!

"It's really nice of you to offer to pay for everything," Alyssa said. "But why don't *we* pay for *you*? As a thank-you for being such a great hostess."

"Yeah!" Grace cried. She turned to the man. "Give her a double extra venti hot dog with nonfat ketchup!"

"Hey, kid, these are hot dogs, not lattes," the man shot back, grinning at Grace. "But I got a foot-long dog that'd feed all four of youse!"

"Only three of us are eating hot dogs," Alyssa said. "I'd like a tofu dog."

"You must be from California," he teased her.

Alyssa smiled. "South Jersey, born and raised."

"Well, *something* went wrong there." He gave her a wink. "One tofu dog, coming right up. And *normal* hot dogs for everybody else?"

"Yes," Jenna said, before Natalie could speak for herself. "And we're paying for hers." She pointed at Natalie. "So don't take any money from her."

"You're the boss," he told Jenna.

The man served up three steaming hot dogs on thick buns, and one tofu dog as well. Alyssa asked for sauerkraut and the others scrunched up their faces and made *yecch* sounds.

Grace stuck her finger in her mouth, pretending to barf as the man heaped the stinky, fermented cabbage on Alyssa's equally disgusting tofu dog.

"Grace, that's so rude," Natalie said, cracking up.

"It's not my best," Grace conceded. "And no one can fake barf like Chelsea."

They all got quiet for a moment as they held their hot dogs. Then Alyssa said, "We'll see Chelsea soon."

Everyone was quiet for a moment.

"Guys," Alyssa said, as she added some spicy brown mustard to her tofu dog. "We made a promise to be nice to her."

There was a group sigh.

"It's gonna be cool," Grace said. "We'll give her the surprise and she will stop being a pain once and for all."

"How are the dogs, girls?" the vendor prompted.

"Great!" Grace made a show of taking a big bite and chewing enthusiastically. "See, Natalie? It doesn't have to be all fancy all the time. It's like camp! Hot dogs bring the world closer together!"

"So does group Chelsea-stressing!" Jenna added. "It's very . . . uniting."

Natalie took a bite of her hot dog. It was good; she couldn't deny that. But she was getting nervous again, and she wasn't sure she would be able to eat very much.

It's all going to be okay, she told herself.

Standing across from her, Alyssa gave her a reassuring smile and quietly ate her tofu dog.

Then Grace said, "Speaking of weird behavior, what was up with Alex and Brynn? Anybody figure that out yet?"

"Not a clue," Jenna replied. She grabbed Grace's wrist and looked at her pink watch. "But we'll find out soon enough."

All of a sudden, Natalie's hot dog tasted like sawdust.

▲ ▲ ▲

"You are gorgeous," Chelsea's dad told her as she modeled her outfit for him. He was sipping chicken noodle soup in bed. He had gotten dressed in a pair of loose jeans and his light blue sweater. He looked pretty good, with some color in his cheeks.

Chelsea had chosen to wear her dark brown burnt-out top with a pair of embroidered jeans. The outfit had been a total score last spring, when he was still working and they had money for clothes.

She stuck out a leg so he could admire the brown-and-silver embroidery on the legs.

"Woo-hoo! All the boys are going to be fighting over you."

"Oh, ick, Daddy," Chelsea said, wrinkling her nose. At his pretend-hurt look, she rolled her eyes. "Boys."

"Hey, *I'm* a boy," he reminded her. "Or I was."

"You're totally not a boy," she insisted. "You're a dad."

"Truer words were never spoken." He laid his soup spoon over his heart. "I am a dad." A huge grin spread across his face. "The best thing to be in the world."

She came up and gave him a big hug. "You're going to be okay if I go, right?"

"Didn't your mom tell you we can't wait for you to get out of our hair?" he chided her. "We're going to party down!"

She gave him a playful smack on the shoulder. Then she cried, "Oh, Daddy! Did I hurt you?"

"No way, dude." He sounded so dorky that she couldn't help but burst out laughing. He laughed too, and cupped her cheek. "Seriously, Chelse. Your mom and I both want you to go and have super-mega fun."

"Okay, I will." She got up off the bed. "Super-mega-ultra fun!"

"You go, girlfriend!" He high-fived her.

Rolling her eyes at him, she left the bedroom.

Soon she and her mom joined the busy weekend traffic. As they left her dad behind in their house, Chelsea felt a mixture of nervousness and total excitement. Okay, those girls were totally immature, but she also wanted to party down with them and have super-mega-ultra fun. There was a part of her—a *big* part—that couldn't wait to eat burgers and show off her outfit and bowl and ride a go-kart.

She thought about her bunk, picturing each girl in her mind. She had actually missed them.

I've grown up a lot, she thought. *Maybe they have, too.*

She really, really wanted to have a good time.

She crossed her fingers for good luck and kept them that way in her lap.

▲ ▲ ▲

Alex was relieved that her mom had called Natalie's mother to tell her that she and Brynn were taking a later bus. That way she hadn't had to talk to Natalie herself. They were going to miss helping decorate the table . . . with *Natalie's* decorations.

That was fine with Alex.

"Are you thinking about Chelsea?" Brynn asked as they rode the bus toward New York City. "You have such a weird look on your face."

"I'm thinking about Natalie," Alex confessed. Her mood darkened. "And *now* I'm thinking about Chelsea."

"I'm stressed out, too," Brynn said. Her eyes got huge. "What if we walk in and Natalie has told everyone we're fighting? And everyone, like, *stares* at us? And the room goes totally silent. The music just stops."

Alex blinked at Brynn's drama-queen version of the situation. It wouldn't be anything like *that*, would it?

Brynn peered at her, staring into her eyes. "Alex? Are you feeling sick?"

Alex shook her head. "I'm great."

"Oh, good." Brynn exhaled. "I thought you were going to say you had to go home."

"No way." Alex took a deep breath and smiled broadly. She would give this reunion her all. She'd make sure she wasn't a drag to anybody, especially not to Brynn.

But how was she going to do that when things were so messed up with Natalie?

▲ ▲ ▲

Jenna, Natalie, Grace, and Alyssa modeled for Natalie's mom, making snobby pout-faces as they stomped down an invisible fashion show runway in the center of the living room. She applauded each girl's strut as they paraded in their cool new outfits.

She'd seen Natalie's choice already, of course. Natalie was wearing a black-and-purple checked top and black leather pants from Italy. Grace was wearing a lavender sweater and black pants, and she had caught up her crazy curls with a stretchy dark purple headband. Jenna was in a purple and gray top and black jeans, which was pretty dressy for her. Alyssa had on her trademark black T-shirt and black jeans. It was awesome with her new haircut.

Natalie's mom had been concerned about Alyssa's short, purple streaks. She was uncertain if Alyssa's mom would be upset that her daughter had done something so extreme when she was away from home. But there wasn't much she could do about it now.

Natalie and the others had decorated the living room for the sleepover. They had crisscrossed strings of plastic palm tree lights across the ceiling. Dark blue and green streamers of seaweed and silly fish with big eyes and kissy lips hung over the windows. Natalie had hung a wacky singing fish mounted on a trophy plaque on the door of the guest bathroom. The robot fish would start to wiggle and sing whenever someone walked past the guest bathroom.

They decided to add Jenna's trunk to the decor, making it look like a little grass shack by draping some green sheets over it. Using Natalie's computer and printer, Jenna made a sign that said FUN SHACK. It was written in a Hawaiian-flower font she found on the Internet. Jenna taped the sign to the entrance to the shack.

With lots of squeals and giggles, they made room for Chelsea's surprise behind the "shack." Then they gathered up several shopping bags brimming with decorations and treats for the bunk table. Each girl had packed some incredible junk food or other goody for everyone else.

"Whoa! That's my sack," Jenna said quickly, as Grace picked up a dark blue bag. "I'll carry it!"

"What's in it?" Grace started to look.

"A surprise," Jenna said quickly. "For the table. So let's go!"

Natalie and the others had permission to enter the party half an hour early to help decorate their table. If Alex and Brynn had made the earlier bus, they would have been included.

Why is Alex so mad at me? Natalie thought anxiously.

The intercom buzzer sounded, and Mr. Bartok said, "Ms. Goode? Is car."

"Thank you, Mr. Bartok," Natalie's mom replied. She rose. "Showtime, ladies. I'll walk you girls outside."

They took the elevator and went through the front door as Mr. Bartok cried, "Ah! You are four beautiful young ladies! The ladies of purple!"

"Have fun," Natalie's mom said, as the four climbed into their car.

Noah placed their bags of goodies into the trunk, got into the driver's seat, and started the engine. The car pulled away.

"I feel like Cinderella!" Grace announced.

"Me too!" Jenna exclaimed, holding her blue bag on her lap.

"Me three," Alyssa murmured. "Thanks for everything, Nat. This has been amazing."

"Yeah, just when I think it can't get any more amazing, it gets more amazing," Grace added.

"It's not over yet," Natalie replied, trying to sound positive. "It'll be so nice to see everybody again."

"Yeah, no kidding. Now you're going to reunite with Prince Charming." Jenna blinked her eyes rapidly, making her eyelashes flutter. She pushed her lips together and made little smooching noises. "Oh, Simon, I *looove* you!"

"Simon! Oh, Simon!" Grace gushed, kissing the back of her own hand.

"Hey, as I recall, you and *Devon* were a thing," Natalie shot back.

"Oh, well," Grace said, all flustered. "He may have competition, you know. Back home."

"Who? Greg? Or Andrew?" all the girls demanded at once. They started teasing Grace about the two boys she hung out with in drama club.

"I wonder if Marissa and Pete will be all lovey-dovey," Grace said, obviously trying to take the attention off herself.

"Love at the reunion! It's so exciting!" Jenna cried.

Everyone laughed hard.

Then the car pulled up to Village Bowl.

"Am I dreaming?" Grace gasped.

Village Bowl took up an entire city block. It was four stories tall and the façade was painted to look like a hip, retro version of Greenwich Village during the fifties. There were all kinds of businesses and stores—a deli, a newspaper stand, a tobacco shop, a bookstore, a beauty parlor, and a soda shoppe.

Painted fifties-style people populated the "buildings." There were guys with oily, slicked-back hair, jeans with rolled-up cuffs, and white T-shirts. Girls in poodle skirts walked by with their noses in the air. One of them was holding a rhinestone-studded leash around the neck of a snooty poodle that was the twin of the one on her dress.

Noah continued down the street, signaling a left, and turned into an underground parking garage. The tunnel was painted to look like a bowling lane, with an explosion of pins on the opposite wall.

"Even the parking garage is amazing!" Grace cried.

Noah pulled into a space in the vast, brightly painted parking area and turned off the engine. He offered to help the girls carry their bags. Natalie thanked him, saying, "We have four sets of hands."

"Besides, the elevator is already here," Jenna announced, grabbing up her mysterious blue bag. She rushed toward the opening doors of an elevator painted like a go-kart zooming toward them. "Hurry, you guys!"

Laughing, the other three caught up with her. All the heavy bags bashed against their knees.

"How's my hair?" Natalie asked Alyssa.

"Perfect," Alyssa assured her. She grinned at her. "*Simon* will love it."

They took the elevator to the fourth floor. When it stopped, an electronic voice shouted, "Get outta here! Have some fun!"

They squealed with laughter.

"We will!" Grace called back.

Before them stood double doors, painted in checks of white, red, and black, with a neon sign over the door that blinked off and on. It read: GET IN HERE! And below it, VILLAGE BOWL PARTY ZONE!

"Here goes nothin'," Jenna said, pushing on the doors. Natalie joined her and they went inside together.

Festive Mylar balloons in all shades of fun bobbed against the ceiling of the Village Bowl Party Room. Metallic streamers hung from the balloons, shimmering in the light of at least three whirling disco balls.

Below the balloons, counselors, CITs, and a few campers were decorating the tables with tablecloths and centerpieces.

"Look!" Jenna jumped up and down, jabbing her finger to the left. Beside an undecorated table, their beloved petite blond counselor was unfolding a shimmery purple tablecloth.

"*Julie!*" all the girls cried at once.

They raced toward her. A clump of balloons at the opposite end of the table moved, and Natalie spotted Marissa behind them.

"Marissa!" she called, waving.

In no time at all, the girls were group-hugging Julie and Marissa. Everyone was talking at once—about their looks—hair, clothes, manicures—and catching up on school, sports, and boys.

Finally, Julie asked them, "Where are Alex and Brynn?"

Jenna, Grace, and Alyssa looked at Natalie, as if she was supposed to speak for the group. She didn't know if she should go into the fight between them. Alex and Brynn weren't here to give their side of the story, and she didn't want to sound like she was tattling on them.

Alyssa stepped up. She said, "Alex needed a little more rest, so they're catching a later bus."

"Oh?" Julie looked concerned. "Is she okay?"

"Yeah," Natalie said. "They're meeting us here."

Julie's frown morphed into a big smile. "All right! That's great news." She resumed unfolding the tablecloth. "Let's hustle. Show me what you brought."

"We got these," Natalie said. She dug in the bag she was holding. Out came a white plastic bowling pin with a slot in the top. Each pin came with a blank name tag to fit into the slot. "We got fourteen of them. They're place cards."

"Cool!" Julie said. "Can a couple of you write the names of all the girls on the cards? We'll put them in a little pile and let each person choose where she wants to sit."

"Can we choose now?" Grace asked. "Because that way, I won't have to sit next to Chel . . . I mean, I'll get to sit with Jenna."

"Yeah, Grace and I have been really wanting to sit next to each other," Jenna added, her eyes big, wide, and innocent as she stood close to Grace. Grace put her arm around Jenna's shoulders.

"We've been totally missing each other," Grace added.

The balloons bumped against each other as Marissa

traded the bunch from her left hand to her right and picked up a Sharpie.

"Now remember, girls," she said. "We want everyone to have a good time, okay? Let's be friendly to everyone."

"*Everyone*," Julie added for emphasis.

"We're on it," Natalie assured her, and the others nodded.

"I'll write the names on the place cards," Alyssa said, taking the Sharpie from Marissa.

"I'll help with that," Grace offered, picking up one of the nametags.

"Great," Julie said, smiling at them. "Now, Natalie, can you help me tape down our tablecloth?"

"Of course," Natalie said, glad to have a good job—one that meant helping Julie.

Marissa said, "Jenna, I want you to tie one balloon to the back of each chair."

Jenna studied the balloons. Then she said slowly, "I wonder what would happen if we tied, like, fifty balloons to one chair. Do you think it would float?"

Marissa clutched the balloons with both hands, keeping them out of Jenna's eager reach.

"That will remain an unanswered question," Marissa ordered her. "Am I clear?"

"Totally," Jenna assured her. She lost her smile and nodded, looking very serious. "Balloon." She pointed to the balloon. "Chair." Pointed to the chair. "I can do that. Promise."

"Okay." With a friendly smile, Marissa handed Jenna the bouquet of balloons. "I'll go get our stash of treats."

"It is *huge*," Julie said.

"*Tell* me you have Twizzlers," Jenna pleaded.

"Wait and see," Julie told her as Marissa dashed away.

"Natalie got little bags of cool stuff from the spa we went to for everyone," Alyssa said, speaking around the pen in her mouth.

Natalie nodded. "Everything is mango."

Julie smiled excitedly. "Oh, that was very thoughtful."

Natalie beamed as she got to work with a container of tape, making loops of the clear sticky stuff and dabbing them against the top of the table. Then she laid the tablecloth over them and pressed down.

"Ingenious!" Julie said approvingly. "If we have tablecloths at the camp social next year, we'll have to do that."

"I've already been thinking up ideas for the social," Natalie told her. "I think it would be fun to do a shipwreck party. My mom said she had one when she was my age. You decorate to make the room look like a tropical island. Then everyone dresses in rags and hula skirts and stuff. I even got a head start on decorations. We bought a bunch of fishy streamers and palm tree lights for the sleepover."

"I'm sure your place looks great," Julie enthused. "It's so nice of you to have an all-bunk sleepover. I wish I could come."

Julie had to leave New York right after the reunion. She was going to a christening in Philadelphia bright and early the next morning.

"I wish you could be there," Natalie replied sincerely.

She wished Julie and Marissa both would be there. But Marissa was going to a Broadway show with some of her girlfriends.

"Natalie, are you okay? You seem a little nervous," Julie said quietly, reaching out and brushing a tendril of hair from out of Natalie's eyes.

Natalie took a breath. "In fact—"

Just then Kathleen, the head of Division Three, called, "Julie! We need you!"

"Natalie, I'm sorry, but I have to go . . . do something," Julie said mysteriously. She waved at Marissa, who was staggering toward the table with three humongous brown plastic trash sacks slung across her back. "It's time!"

Marissa nodded back. "Okay. Here, guys." She bent over gratefully as Grace, Jenna, and Alyssa retrieved the heavy sacks. "We'll be back in a little while."

"Wow, what is in here?" Grace asked, setting down her sack on a chair and opening it. "Purple Pixy Stix!" she announced. "And grape gum! *And* Twizzlers!"

Everyone cheered.

Together Julie and Marissa trotted across the room. Jenna's sister Stephanie and Lizzie, the counselor from 3A, hurried to join the other counselors and CITs. Natalie spotted Brian, the cute sports counselor from Australia; Bethany, the drama instructor; and Kathleen, the head of the third division, as they all disappeared through a brightly decorated door.

"Those guys are up to something," Natalie said.

"Yeah." Jenna grinned. "I wish I were in on it."

"Do you know what it is?" Grace asked Jenna. "Did Stephanie tell you?"

Jenna shook her head.

"Well, we'll find out soon enough," Grace reminded them. "We only have twenty minutes left until the reunion officially starts."

Natalie's heart raced. "Eek! You guys!" she cried. "We have so got to concentrate on getting our table ready." She whipped out the zebra-print sunglasses from her bag of decorations. "I'm not sure these actually go with our theme," she said.

"They do," Alyssa said. She put on her pair. "They're totally fun and retro. Like Village Bowl."

"Here's the snack tray," Grace said, pulling a large white tray out of one of the sacks. "And the stickers." She showed them the packets of purple alphabet stickers.

The plan was to put everyone's name on the tray in purple sticker letters. Alyssa said, "Grace, I'll work on the tray while you get the place cards finished. Nat, how about you put the sunglasses in the spa gift bags?"

"Okay. And I'll get all the snacks from Julie and Marissa's trash bags out on the table," Jenna said.

Jenna pulled out gobs of sour apple candy, Skittles, lots and lots of Hershey's Kisses, and a wide assortment of sugar-free candy from the trash bags.

"I think most of our bunk is bringing goodies," Alyssa said, looking up from tearing open a packet of alphabet stickers. "Maybe we should have brought more trays."

"You have a point," Natalie said.

There were also little bottles of body glitter, and really goofy stuffed animals—bugs with big glasses and birds with buckteeth—that they also put into the spa bags.

Shortly after that, Julie and Marissa reappeared.

Julie said, "Girls, you have done a fantastic job! Our table is a fantasy come true."

The four bunkmates, Julie, and Marissa stepped back to admire the purple table laden with wonderful treats for all the girls of 3C. Natalie was so proud that tears actually welled in her eyes.

Marissa looked at her and said, "Natalie, your eye makeup is running."

"Oh, *no!*" Natalie cried, touching her face. "Which way to the bathroom?"

"They're over there," Julie said, pointing to the left. Two bowling-pin doors were labeled GUYS and GALS. "Let's all go. Last-minute check before our big show."

They headed for the bathroom. Then Jenna slowed, saying, "Whoops, I forgot my . . . purse. Be right there."

The others crowded into the girls' bathroom. Natalie reapplied her eyeliner and Marissa sprayed body glitter on her neck and arms. Grace sprayed some of the glitter on her hair.

"Oh, that looks good!" Julie said, nodding as Grace twirled in a circle.

Music began to play. Julie said, "It's time to party, girls!"

Just then Jenna pushed into the bathroom, panting and fanning her face.

"Hey," she said.

"Where's your purse?" Julie asked.

"What?" Jenna rolled her eyes. "Oh, no, I forgot it *again!*"

"Jenna Bloom," Marissa said suspiciously. "You're up to something."

"Me?" Jenna asked, her eyes wide and innocent. "Never!"

Julie folded her arms. "I think Marissa's right, Jenna. You're planning a prank."

Just then the bathroom door opened. 3C bunkmates Sarah and Candace sailed into the bathroom!

Everyone shrieked and hugged one another.

"This is so cool!" Sarah cried, jumping up and down. She had on really cute plastic bowling pin earrings. She was dressed in a yellow sweater and black pants, and Candace, her brown hair still cropped short, had on dark green all the way.

"It's so cool!" Candace echoed.

Natalie had forgotten Candace's habit of repeating everything everyone else said. She was so amazingly glad to see Sarah and Candace both.

"I didn't have anything purple," Sarah apologized, looking at Natalie's outfit.

"Me neither," Candace said.

"Who cares?" Grace said. "You're here and that's what counts!"

Julie hugged the two new arrivals tightly and said, "And you both look so good! But listen, ladies, we can't have our bunk reunion in the bathroom. Let's go back to our table."

"Yeah! Everyone is showing up at once," Sarah said. "I saw Karen walking in."

"Karen's here, too!" Candace echoed.

"Um, has anyone seen Simon?" Natalie asked.

"Pfft. You've seen one boy, you've seen 'em all," Jenna retorted. Then she giggled and added, "No Simon yet, but *Devon* is here, *Grace*."

"Oooh, it's love!" Sarah teased.

"You guys!" Grace protested. But she looked really happy to hear that Devon had shown.

I can't wait to see Simon, Natalie thought. She pushed open the door and dashed out.

And crashed right into Alex!

chapter TEN

Alex staggered backward and fell against Brynn as Natalie rammed into her. She could tell by Natalie's shocked expression that Natalie hadn't meant to do it.

But Alex was so startled that she said, "Hey, watch it!"

Natalie's mouth opened, but whatever she was going to say—hopefully, "I'm sorry I took over the whole reunion"—was interrupted by the other bunkmates. With cries of joy, they both gave Alex and Brynn big, tight, warm, fuzzy hugs.

"Oh, it's so good to see you two!" Julie cried. "You both look so great! How was the bus ride?"

"Okay," Alex said. "Long."

"It was nerve-wracking, wondering if we would be able to come," Brynn added.

"Not come?" Marissa asked.

Brynn nodded. "Yeah, because of Alex feeling sick."

Alex reddened as all gazes turned to her. She knew Brynn hadn't meant to embarrass her—Brynn was just being her usual dramatic self—but she was embarrassed anyway.

"I'm *fine*." Alex didn't mean to sound so mean.

Julie piped up and said, "Let's go back to our table."

Alex just nodded. She did have to go to the bathroom—that's why she had been headed *for* the bathroom—but she could wait.

She knew she hadn't spoken to Grace, Jenna, or Alyssa yet. She didn't know what to say. And as for Natalie, it was probably better if she didn't say anything more at all.

On the other hand, she was finally at the reunion. She waved at Jessie, who was coming through the double doors with hundreds of other Lakeview campers. Alex had been looking forward to this moment ever since she'd received the invitation, and she almost hadn't gotten to come. But it felt like it was all ruined . . . and it hadn't even started yet.

As they reached the Bunk 3C table, Alex took in all the decorations that *other people* had arranged. She thought it looked like a mish-mash. There were bowling-themed items, and things that didn't go together at all except that they were purple. There was a tray covered with purple letters containing more candy than she had ever seen, including on Halloween.

To her right, Bunk 3A jumped to their feet and booed the appearance of 3C. Marta, Gaby, Christa, and Jill were going way overboard in their boos and grimaces. 3A and 3C were traditional Camp Lakeview rivals. Gaby, who had briefly buddied up to Grace, stuck out her tongue. Christa and Jill copied her.

Bunk 3A's table was decorated in Color War blue

.d red, and it looked great. They even had the same napkins that she had purchased!

Maybe I should go sit with them, Alex thought, not even joining in as her bunkmates dissed 3A back. She still couldn't get over that their enemy bunk went with her idea, while her own bunk didn't.

She randomly pulled out a chair to sit down at the 3C table. Then she realized that there were name cards at each place. There were six places on each side, and one on each end. The end places were for Julie and Marissa. But Alex had been seated between Natalie and Chelsea.

Would she have to spend the entire party sitting next to Natalie? So Natalie could spend the entire reunion explaining to Alex why her decorations were better?

And why did *she* have to sit next to Chelsea? Chelsea was the last one on the row, with Marissa seated to her right at the end.

"Look! There are little bottles of stuff from Natalie's fancy spa in these bags!" Sarah announced as she picked up a bag labeled SARA. They even misspelled Sarah's name! Didn't they care about anything except getting their own way?

"Hey, these cards are all messed up," Grace announced, as she and the others started moving around the table, looking for their names. "They're not at the places we put them."

Jenna grimaced. "Sorry about that. I kind of knocked them over when I was looking for my, um, purse. I couldn't remember where they went."

"We're all bunkmates," Sarah said. "So it doesn't matter where we sit. Or, um, if our names are misspelled.

Besides, I plan to bowl and race go-karts most of the time! Not sit around!"

"And the boy-crazy girls will be off kissing and dancing," Brynn added.

"Look! There's Karen!" Jenna cried.

Soon everyone except Valerie and Chelsea had gathered at the table. Natalie sat next to Alex and looked straight ahead. She didn't speak to Alex, and Alex didn't say a word to her, either. The others were trying on their purple sunglasses and putting on nail tattoos and having a good time. All the cool stuff was from Natalie.

Alex felt even more like a total loser.

A DJ wearing a big beige hat was sitting at a console that read DJ KMAXX! He smiled as Kathleen walked up to him with a piece of paper. Probably a song request, Alex realized. The DJ nodded and punched something in to his console.

As the girls sat down, the spicy smells of pizza, hamburgers, hot dogs, and French fries filled the air. Although it reminded her of camp, Alex didn't feel hungry in the least. And she sure didn't feel like dancing, even if the songs were the latest and greatest.

Marissa and Julie brought over large pitchers of soda, one in each hand, and set them down on the table.

"This one's Diet Coke," Julie told Alex as she placed it in front of her.

Alex nodded. Even though she knew a lot of the other girls drank diet sodas, she felt singled out.

Just then, Dr. Steve appeared on the little stage at the end of the room. He was wearing his navy blue Camp Lakeview polo shirt and khakis. In fact, he looked the same as he did at camp, except he was a little pale, compared to his usual burnt-lobster hue at camp.

Everyone at the table except Alex, Marissa, and Julie started cheering and screaming. Alex just sat there.

"Hello, Camp Lakeview alumni!" Dr. Steve said. The microphone zinged and he took a step away from it. Then he craned his neck down and said, "Can you hear me now?"

Laughter echoed off the walls.

"Okay, let's review some safety tips and Village Bowl regulations, and then we'll get this reunion started."

More applause and cheers rocked the house. Alex heard some boys hooting and strained to see where 3F was sitting. But she couldn't see beyond the 3C table. They had so much stuff heaped on it that it blocked her view of the rest of the party room.

Their beloved leader started to blink as he droned a long list of rules and regulations, most of it seeming to center around wearing socks with their rented bowling shoes. As was their habit, the girls of 3C pretty much ignored "Dr. Flutter Bug," which was his camp nickname because he blinked so much.

Then Dr. Steve finally said, "All right! Our DJ, KMAXX, will be taking requests, so just come up and tell him what you want to hear. And now, I declare this reunion officially begun!"

Everyone yelled and cheered again. Alex couldn't find it in her heart to say one "yay."

"That means we can start eating, right?" Grace asked Julie.

"Yes," Julie said. "It's a buffet, so you can grab a plate and load up on whatever you want. I'll bet Jenna will eat at least four burgers. Right, Jenna?"

But Jenna didn't reply. She was studying 3A's table as if something was wrong. Alex wondered if she thought the Color War theme was dumb, too.

"I'm eating six pieces of pizza," Sarah announced. "What about you, Alex?"

"Sure," Alex muttered. She started to push back her chair at the exact same time as Natalie. She got her ankle caught in her chair leg and fell forward—knocking over the pitcher of Diet Coke. It splashed all over Sarah, completely soaking her from her chest on down.

"Oh, no!" Sarah wailed, leaping to her feet. She was dripping wet. She staggered backward, staring at herself, and burst into tears. "My outfit!"

"I'm so sorry!" Alex cried. "Let me help you!"

Sarah ran for the bathroom. Alex started to follow, but Julie said, "Don't worry, Alex. I'll handle it."

Julie took off after Sarah while the rest of the table immediately started cleaning up the mess. Alex gathered up wads of napkin to sop up the huge pool of soda on the table.

Then Jenna said, "Hmm, oh, dear," and frowned over at 3A's table again.

Then all of a sudden, some of the 3A girls erupted into a humongous argument.

Marta yelled, "Just stop it!" at Gaby.

Gaby shouted back, "Oh, just get over yourself!"

"Girls, girls!" Lizzie cried. She started talking to them in a low voice.

Maybe she can come over here next and straighten us out, Alex thought.

Next, wild music and screeching singing blared from the center of 3A's table! It drowned out Lizzie, and all the girls started shouting and covering their ears. It was some crazy hip-hop song—and it sounded like Jenna was singing the words!

> *"Bunk 3A, yo, 3A!*
> *I see that bunk, I run away!*
> *Ooh, ooh, they so fresh!*
> *They put 3C to the test!*
> *Bunk 3A! I'm singing 3A, yo!"*

"Oh, this is *so* not working out the way I planned it!" Jenna cried.

Around the party room, most of the other party-goers were cracking up, hooting and laughing. Alex couldn't help the lopsided grin that crossed her face. Jenna had pulled another prank that was spinning out of control!

"Something's under the table!" Gaby cried.

As Alex watched in stunned amazement, Jenna dashed over to 3A and dove under their table at the same time that half the bunk did the same. There was a lot of yelling. Jenna disappeared. Then she crawled back out, holding her laptop in her arms!

Gaby and Marta, and some of the other 3A bunkmates headed straight for Jenna as Jenna ran back to 3C's table.

The music stopped playing just as Gaby yelled, "Knock it off!"

"Help!" Jenna cried, running around to Alex's side of the table.

At the same time, the DJ started playing the old song, "YMCA" by the Village People. The laughter died down as everybody waited to see what would happen next.

Stephanie and Lizzie trotted toward the center of the room. So did many of the other counselors.

"Jenna, you are so busted!" Marissa warned Jenna. Then she said to Alex, "I guess Julie is still helping Sarah. Can you girls work on the spill?"

"Yes," Alex assured her.

"Do not go anywhere, Jenna," Marissa said.

Then she reached beneath the table, grabbed something made out of navy blue material, and ran to join the others. She was holding a fishing hat just like Dr. Steve always wore at camp, and as the girls started laughing, she put it on. All the other counselors and CITs put on fishing hats, too!

They sang along with the music:

"Campers! Are you longing for home?
I say, campers! Did you bring a cell phone?
Hey guess what! Now that I'm grown I can
serve you breakfast!
Cuz I am a C-I-T!"
The chorus kicked in:
"Camp C-I-T!
I used to be a Camp C-I-T!"

The place went nuts as the counselors and former

CITs did a funky version of the Electric Slide. Then they pulled Dr. Steve, Nurse Helen, Kathleen, and all the other division heads onto the floor. Some of the older campers began to dance.

"This is awesome!" Grace cried. "It's like they copied Jenna!"

"They did!" Jenna said. "I came up with a funny song first!"

"Yeah, and now 3A is out for revenge," Grace said as their rivals glared at them. Alex guessed that the only reason they hadn't stomped over to 3C was because Lizzie had told them not to.

The YMCA-CIT song ended. The dancers all swept a low bow and started applauding all the campers. Everyone at the tables clapped, whistled, and hooted back.

It was crazy, and despite herself, Alex started grinning broadly. She loved her Camp Lakeview family. She really did.

Suddenly, right beside her, Gaby's voice filled the room, yelling, "Knock it off! Knock it off! Knock it off!" in a loop on Jenna's laptop.

Everyone started laughing again—except bunk
3A. And Kathleen, and Nurse Helen, and Dr. Steve.

Jenna swallowed hard and said, "How did *that*
happen?" as she worked the keyboard of her laptop
and shut it down. She looked freaked out.

Dr. Steve himself walked up to Jenna and said,
"Please come with me."

Jenna followed behind him as he led her to a
corner of the room. He began to talk and gesture at
her laptop. Jenna's head was bowed.

"Wow, he looks mad," Natalie said.

"I'm so glad I'm not Jenna," Grace chimed in.

Marissa got up and joined them, her arms
crossed over her chest. Nurse Helen and Kathleen
went over with them as well.

Then Marissa walked Jenna back to the table,
carrying Jenna's laptop for her.

"Wow, that was an awesome prank!" Grace said.

"Dr. Steve didn't think so," Jenna sulked. "That
man has no sense of humor."

"Gaby was very embarrassed, Jenna," Marissa
said.

"But I told you guys, that wasn't part of the prank!" She turned to her bunkmates. "See, what happened, was I made a funny song with Nicole," Jenna explained. "My new friend back home. Then I recorded it onto my laptop. I recorded a bunch of blank songs first, so I could delay the song, and then I hid it under 3A's table."

"That was why you had to carry your blue bag. Your laptop was in it," Grace guessed.

"Yeah, and then when I said I went to get my purse, that's when I saw my chance to hide it under there. But then when Alex spilled the pitcher of soda all over Sarah, I got worried that something might happen to it. Then it went off!"

She looked at Marissa. "Like I said, I didn't mean to record Gaby mouthing off. I must have hit the record button or something when I was trying to get away."

"Oh, Jenna Bloom," Marissa said, shaking her head. "You have a gift for turning a small prank into total chaos."

"I hate to tell you this, Marissa," Natalie said, "but I think Jenna will take that as a compliment."

That's exactly what I was thinking! Alex thought. All at once, she was confused about how she felt about Natalie. She was really mad at her, but she felt so weird sitting next to her not saying anything. And then Natalie had gone and said the exact same words that Alex had thought of saying. It made her remember how close they had once been. Part of her was totally glad to see her again. Even if she was angry.

I wish I could hit the rewind button and start this whole thing over, Alex thought sadly.

As everyone sat back down, Julie and Sarah returned

to the table. Sarah was wearing a black-and-white skirt and a black sweater. They were a little baggy on her, but it was a good outfit. She looked totally stylish.

"Julie is lending me the clothes she's wearing to the christening tomorrow," Sarah said happily.

"You look hot," Natalie said.

"Jenna got in trouble while you were gone," Marissa told Julie. "She hid her laptop under 3A's table and then accidentally recorded and played back Gaby."

"Yeah, Gaby having a spazz attack!" Grace said, and Jenna tried not to smile. "Everyone heard it!"

Julie groaned. "Jenna Bloom, I swear! You're shortening my life."

"I'm sorry, Julie," Jenna said sincerely. "It's just . . . so easy for me," she finished with a sigh.

"Our table is falling into chaos!" Brynn cried. "What shall we do?"

"Maybe we should eat," Grace suggested.

The girls started to get in line for burgers and pizza slices. Alex stayed where she was.

As they came back with food, Julie sat down in Chelsea's empty chair.

"Alex, is something wrong?" Julie asked kindly. "You don't seem like you're having very much fun."

Alex shook her head. Then she decided to be honest. She said, "I really liked my Color War idea. I thought it would be funny if both 3A and 3C did it, because we could challenge each other to see who did the theme better. Then it would *be* like a Color War."

"Oh." Julie looked impressed. "That *would* have been really fun."

"Yeah, and Brynn thought so, too," Alex continued. "But you guys wouldn't listen. As soon as Natalie said 'purple,' there was nothing more to say."

"No way," Grace chimed in as she returned to the table with her plate of food. "No one spoke up, so Julie figured we all agreed on purple."

Alex looked up to see that many of the others had also returned with their food. Natalie stood between Alyssa and Grace, listening carefully.

"I *wanted* to do the Color War idea," Karen said.

"Yeah, really," Candace added.

"Oh, Alex, I'm so sorry," Julie said.

"No wonder you got so annoyed at Natalie," Grace exclaimed. Then she covered her face with her hands. "Eek. Forget I said that."

"Well, if Alex thought everyone had been ignoring her, no wonder she sent that snarky IM," Jenna said.

"It was *not* snarky," Alex said, mortified. As Brynn gave her a look, she mumbled, "Okay. Maybe it was."

"It *so* was!" Grace said. "We were all like, 'What happened to Alex?'"

"Just because I was trying so hard to make things nice for everyone," Natalie added. Her voice was shaking.

"You took it all over!" Alex cried.

"Talk about a Color War," Jenna said. "This is like a bunk war."

"Total war," Candace echoed.

"Okay, time out," Julie said. She looked from Alex to Natalie to Marissa.

"Alex, no one meant to ignore your suggestions," Julie reassured Alex. "Maybe if you had had a chance to explain your idea about challenging 3A, we would have stuck with Color War. I'm sorry I didn't pay better attention."

"It's not your fault," Alex said to Julie. Tears sprang to her eyes and she tried to blink them away. "If anything, I *should* have persisted, like you said. That's been my problem in soccer, too. I give up too soon."

"Alex thought at first that you *had* agreed to the Color War idea," Brynn said. "She spent all her allowance on napkins and stuff for the table. And then she couldn't even return them."

"Oh, did you bring them?" Natalie asked, her voice rising with excitement. "Because I totally didn't buy enough for the sleepover tonight."

"Because *I* totally dumped my pizza all over her mom's carpet," Grace moaned. "And used up the ones at her house."

"It's no biggie," Natalie said. But her cheeks were pink.

Alex knew Natalie like having things perfect. Having pizza dumped on her mom's carpet had probably really upset her. Alex wondered if there had been other mishaps as well.

Maybe it hasn't been total fun 24/7 for Nat, either, Alex thought. But she still felt hurt and angry.

"Everyone is totally stressing," Brynn announced. It was the kind of thing Brynn lived to say.

"You girls haven't been around one another for a while," Julie pointed out. "I'm sure everyone has been a little nervous about getting together. Remember what it was like the first couple of days at camp?"

"Well, that would be about ten million years ago for Alex," Jenna said. "She's been a Camp Lakeview camper forever."

"I hated it," Natalie admitted. "I wanted to go home. No offense, you guys."

"I wasn't very into it, either," Alyssa put in.

"But we learned to get along," Marissa said. "And we had an awesome summer, didn't we?"

"Yeah, we did," Grace said.

"Well, it looks like we've kind of forgotten how to get along," Sarah ventured.

The others nodded.

"We're back together for the first time in a long time," Grace said. "Plus, I don't know about everybody else, but I was pretty hyper about coming to the reunion."

"I couldn't even decide what to wear," Karen said.

"Me, neither," Candace said.

"I'll bet Natalie's been trying very hard to make sure everyone has fun at her house," Julie continued.

"She's got these *lists!*" Grace announced, mimicking trying to hold up a huge weight. Natalie turned bright red, and Alex couldn't help but feel a little sorry for her.

Before she realized what she was saying, Alex said, "I was a nervous wreck having just Brynn over."

Brynn stared at her. "You were nervous having *me* over? Why? I'm just me!"

Alex turned to her. "Because Natalie's was where the fun was. They were going to the art show and having a spa day. I saw your guidebook to New York. You really wanted to be here, not stuck at my house!"

Brynn blurted, "That's not true!" Then she took a breath. "Wait a sec. That's kind of true."

Alex was stunned. "*What?*" she cried.

"She said it was kind of true," Candace said helpfully.

Brynn nodded. "I can't lie about that. I was afraid I was missing out. But I told myself that at least I'd get to watch you play extreme soccer."

Alex shut her eyes tightly as she made a face. "And then I didn't wake you up."

"Wow, this is totally messed up," Grace said.

"Well, let's do a do-over," Julie suggested. "After all, we're 3C! We're the cool bunk!"

"That's right! The cool bunk!" Candace said.

Just then Julie's cell phone rang. She connected and held it to her ear. "Hello? Oh." Her face fell. "Oh, dear, I'm so sorry. We'll miss you."

Alex looked around the table. Only Valerie and Chelsea were missing.

Alex sensed the relief going all around the table. Also the guilt. Because people were thinking, *Maybe Chelsea's the one who's not going to show.*

"Well, everyone says hi, Valerie," Julie said into the phone. "We'll take lots of pictures and upload them so you can share in the fun."

Julie hung up and put her cell phone into her purse. She cocked her head and sighed as she gazed at each bunkmate of 3C in turn.

"Valerie can't make it. She's got the flu."

No one said anything. But Alex knew what they were thinking. Because even though she was ashamed of herself, she was thinking it too: Why couldn't it have been *Chelsea* who wasn't coming? Because they were already having enough trouble getting along. Add Chelsea to the equation and it would equal majorly strained nerves.

"I was kind of hoping it would be Chelsea," Grace finally admitted.

A look passed from girl to girl, and Julie sighed heavily.

"Look, you guys promised to be nice to Chelsea," Julie said, sounding frustrated with them.

"You all know that Chelsea's father is really sick," Marissa put in. "She almost didn't come because she's so worried about him."

"We know. And we feel bad," Natalie said.

"Yeah, movie-star bad. So bad you lounged around all day at a spa," Alex retorted. She meant it as a joke, but it fell way flat. Natalie looked crushed.

"Gee, thanks, Alex," she snapped.

"Girls, *please!*" Julie implored them. "You just made up! Look at how much pressure you're under. It's making you so touchy. Think about what it must be like for Chelsea."

"You're right," Alex said. "We need to make a special effort to be nice to Chelsea. Even though she's not always nice to us."

"That's better," Julie said. "And . . . ?" she prompted Alex.

Alex smiled sheepishly at Natalie. "I'm sorry. I was trying to make a joke. But it didn't work."

"Hey, that's okay." Natalie smiled shyly back. "I'm sorry that everything's gotten so weird between us, Alex. I really am. And we'll make a super gi-normous effort, Julie. We promise."

As she spoke, Karen, who was sitting across from her, caught her breath and looked up past the top of Alex's head.

"Why?" said a tight, angry voice behind Alex. A very familiar voice. "Because it's so *hard* to be nice to me?"

Swallowing, Alex turned in her chair and tilted back her head.

Chelsea was standing right behind her!

And she was glaring so hard at Alex and Natalie, it was like flames were shooting from her eyes.

chapter
TWELVE

"Chelsea, hi," Natalie and Alex said breathlessly as they got to their feet. The rest of the bunk quickly did the same. "It's—it's so good to see you."

"Yeah, right," Chelsea snapped.

Her blond hair was perfect. Her makeup was flawless. And her outfit was fantastic.

But the look on her face ruined it.

Then Julie and Marissa moved around Natalie and Alex and gathered her up in a hug. Exchanging guilty looks, Natalie and Alex joined the huddle.

I can't believe Chelsea heard us, Natalie thought. Alex's expression seemed to say the same thing.

"How was the drive into the city?" Marissa asked her. She looked around the room. "Is your mom still here?"

"No, she dropped me off," Chelsea said. She was looking at the table. She saw something that made her frown, but she didn't say what it was.

"Let's go get a plate for you," Julie offered. "We just sat down to eat."

"We have all kinds of soda, too," Natalie said eagerly. "Can I pour you some?"

"There must be diet, if Alex is drinking soda," Chelsea said.

"Well, there was!" Grace laughed nervously. "Alex kind of used it all up!"

Everyone started to giggle out of their awkward tension, and not so much because they thought it was funny.

"Is this some kind of in-joke I'm not supposed to get?" Chelsea asked. Her voice was so sharp, it was like a knife.

"I knocked it over and spilled it all over Sarah," Alex explained.

"I'm wearing Julie's clothes," Sarah put in.

"Oh, that explains why they look about six sizes too big," Chelsea said. She added, "Where am I supposed to sit? In front of the dumb-looking bowling ball that has my name spelled all wrong?"

Alex glanced at Chelsea's name card on the plastic bowling ball. It read *CHESLEA.*

"Oh, I'm sorry," Grace said, taking it from her and shaking her head. "I wrote that. I got it mixed up. We were hurrying and—"

"I should have known. I mean, you have trouble reading, right? So of course you can't spell either," Chelsea interrupted.

Grace blinked. She looked stunned. Everyone else just stared at Chelsea. They couldn't believe how rude she was being.

"Let's feed you," Julie said quickly. She smiled at Chelsea and led her away from the table.

"Yeah, because I think she has low blood sugar," Alex muttered.

"Wow, she's cranky even for Chelsea," Natalie said.

"Way cranky," Candace said.

"Well, you know she heard us talking about her," Alex reminded Natalie.

Natalie winced. "I feel awful."

"Me, too," Alex confessed.

"Make that three," Grace added.

"Four," Jenna put in.

"Well, let's have a do-over *again* and try to have a good time," Natalie suggested. "My mom says that a good mood can be contagious."

"Okay, let's try," Alex said.

They started talking and eating. The dance beat picked up. Natalie's toes were tapping and she wondered again where Simon was. Then, almost as if he had heard her thought . . . there he was, grinning down at her!

Wow! Simon had grown at least four inches since she had last seen him! His face was thinner, too. His eyes, just as amazingly blue, surrounded by his jet black hair. He had on a black leather jacket, a black T-shirt, and jeans. He looked like a rock star.

"Hey, Natalie," he said. His voice made rockets go off all up and down her spine. Her cheeks tingled. "How are you?"

"Great," she said.

"Oh, *Simon*," Grace teased. "Natalie totally missed you!"

"I like your hair," he said.

Natalie flushed. Then Simon said, "Would you like to dance?"

Dance? With Simon? Of course! She had only been daydreaming about it for six months!

"Okay." Somehow she managed to get up out of her chair.

He took her hand and electricity sizzled through her fingertips. She ignored the giggles behind them as they walked to the dance floor.

It was a fast dance, so they started moving to the hip-hop beat. Simon was a great dancer. That was cool. A lot of boys weren't very good dancers.

The song ended and the beat changed. Natalie recognized the new song as a sort of techno version of the theme song of her dad's latest movie. Simon recognized it, too, and he grinned at her.

"Freaky," he said, and she nodded. Then his grin became a wonderful smile and he took her hands and put them on his shoulders.

They danced for a long time. She saw Grace and Devon, and Alex with Adam . . . hmm, maybe something was heating up between those two! But what about that eighth-grader, Peter, who liked her?

Then she saw Marissa and her own crush, dark-headed, ponytailed Pete, making goo-goo eyes at each other, standing off to one side holding drinks and talking.

All the songs were fast, and Natalie wondered if the grown-ups had planned it that way.

Finally Simon said, "I'm thirsty."

"We have soda at my table," Natalie said.

They walked hand-in-hand back toward the table. Some of the other girls were missing, but Chelsea was there, nibbling on a piece of pizza. She looked no happier than before.

Natalie assumed the other girls were getting more food or dancing. Dr. Steve had explained that the first hour of the reunion was for eating and mixing, and then they would be free to explore the rest of Village Bowl—watch Josie's movie, or bowl, or race go-karts.

"Hi, Natalie! Hey, Simon," Pete said as he and Marissa caught up with the two campers. "I think you're headed our way."

"It's so good to see you," Natalie said to Pete. "How have you been?"

"Great." Pete looked relaxed and happy, the way he usually looked. Except maybe when he had just burnt all the French toast. "Especially since I didn't have to do any of the cooking for the party."

Everyone laughed. "Yeah, that makes us pretty happy, too," Simon jibed. Natalie noticed his use of the word "us" and she thought that was extremely cool.

They reached the table. Pete smiled broadly at Chelsea and said, "Hey, how you doing, Chelsea? Long time no see."

"Only six months. That's not all that long," she said in a flat voice. She didn't stand up to hug him or anything.

Pete was cool, though. He sat down in Marissa's chair and faced Chelsea, his hands between his knees. Marissa sat on the other side and Natalie and Simon took Julie and Grace's chairs.

"Did you have any trouble getting to the reunion?" he asked.

"Just trouble deciding whether or not I should bother to come," she replied. She kept eating her pizza.

"Well, I'm glad you did," Pete replied.

Chelsea shifted in her chair. Natalie caught her glancing toward the dance floor, and on impulse, she whispered to Simon, "Would you ask her to dance?"

He raised his brows. She nodded encouragingly.

"If you want me to," he whispered back. "She does seem kind of lonely." He cleared his throat. "Hey, Chelsea, would you like to dance?"

She gave him a withering glance. "I only dance with cool boys."

Simon's face turned bright red. Natalie was just about to let Chelsea have it for being so rude when Adam and Alex came trotting over. Alex looked flushed from dancing.

They both said hi to everyone at the table and then Adam asked Natalie, "Is it true my sister got herself delivered to your apartment building in a *trunk?*"

"He doesn't believe me!" Alex informed them.

Natalie giggled. Then she pointed as Jenna came skipping back to the table nibbling on a big piece of chocolate cake. "Ask her!" She turned to Simon. "Let's go bowling and ride go-karts!"

"You're on," he said.

Natalie glanced over at Chelsea. Her head was tucked down as she steadily ate her pizza. She seemed so uncomfortable that Natalie felt sorry for her, despite how rude she had been to Simon—and everyone else. She wanted to say to her, "Please just relax and have a good time. We want to be friends with you. You'll see later at my house that we really want you to be happy."

But she was hesitant to talk to her at that moment. She was afraid Chelsea would just twist whatever she had to say and try to hurt her feelings.

So she regretfully walked past her with Simon. Then they pushed through the double doors, laughing and giggling, and headed for the elevators. Bowling was on the next floor down, and the go-karts were on the lowest floor.

"What shall we do first?" Natalie asked Simon.

"Everything!" Simon replied, and they both cracked up.

▲ ▲ ▲

The rest of the reunion was a blur. Natalie and Simon ran into everyone from the bunk, either bowling or riding go-karts, and watching part of Josie's movie (Natalie had already seen it at a sneak screening at her dad's over Christmas break). It was like a wonderful dream that went by all too fast.

Before she knew it, she had hugged and said good-bye to Julie and Marissa. Then Simon walked with her to the two limos her mother had hired to transport the girls of Bunk 3C to Natalie's apartment. The seven girls who had come straight to the reunion had their suitcases and sleeping bags with them. The limo drivers quickly stored their luggage and instructed the girls where to find the sodas and snacks.

"We know the drill!" Grace said airily. She waved her hands at Natalie as she popped out of the moon roof. "C'mon, Goode, let's kick it!"

Simon and Natalie faced each other. The girls hung out of the two limos making kissing noises and chanting, "Natalie and Simon, sitting in a tree. K-I-S-S-I-N-G!"

They both tried to ignore the others. "It was so awesome to see you," Simon said to Natalie. "Maybe we could hang out over spring break?"

Natalie didn't know how she managed not to shout "*Yes!*" Instead, she said warmly, "I'd like that."

"Cool." His smile was shy. The girls in the limos whistled and cheered.

Wincing, Natalie grinned back and said, "I have a sleepover to host."

"You'll do great," he said, and she realized that he knew she was nervous even though she hadn't told him.

"I hope so," she confessed.

He gave her a quick wink and squeezed her hand. All her bunkmates made groaning and barfing noises. "I have complete faith in you, Natalie."

"Thanks." Her hand was tingling. So was her face.

She turned and climbed into the first limo. Grace, Jenna, Alyssa, Karen, and Chelsea were already seated. She was disappointed that Alex was in the other limo, because she wanted to ask her how it had gone with Adam.

Chelsea still looked as miserable as ever. Natalie was a little nervous about Karen sitting beside Chelsea, because Chelsea had really pushed her around at camp.

Everyone except Chelsea yakked and helped themselves to sodas and pretzels. Karen offered a handful of pretzels to Chelsea, who said, "I'm not hungry." She could have said, "No thank you," or "Maybe in a little bit." But, no. Chelsea had to be superblunt and kind of mean about it.

Grace, Jenna, and Alyssa gazed at Natalie as if they

were all thinking the same thing she was. But no one said anything. Everyone pretended not to notice Chelsea's rudeness, just as Pete, Julie, and the other people at the party had overlooked it as well.

"That was so fun," Karen said. "I went to a bowling birthday party a few weeks ago, but it was nothing like this!"

"Bowling parties are so over," Chelsea snapped. "Get a clue, Karen."

Natalie started to seethe, but Alyssa gave her a look that said, "Chill."

Before anyone could say anything more, Chelsea looked at Natalie and said, "I hope we're not going to stay up all night. I'm really tired."

Then why did you come? Natalie wanted to ask her. But she held back, muttering, "I think I'll have some pretzels."

She had been right to worry about tonight's sleepover. Chelsea was going to do everything in her power to ruin it.

▲ ▲ ▲

It had begun to snow by the time the two limos stopped at the curb in front of Natalie's building. The doors flew open before the drivers could get to them, and all eleven girls tumbled out, laughing and catching snowflakes on their tongues.

Chelsea thought about her mother, throwing back her head and pretending to taste delicious flavors. Her hands were sweating. She didn't know how to explain to the others how scared she was. All she could think to do was try to stay as calm as possible. And to stay calm, she needed these noisy, immature girls to be quiet for a while.

As if, she thought angrily. *I can't believe how silly and loud they're being!*

▲ ▲ ▲

The entire bunk managed to cram into the elevator and zoom up to Natalie's apartment. Natalie's mom was out, and would be back at midnight. As with the Friday night sleepover, all the parents had consented to let the girls stay alone because Natalie's neighbor, Mrs. Goldberg, was available in case of emergencies.

Alex was astounded at how fancy Natalie's apartment was. She had known that Natalie's family was very wealthy, but it was like being in a movie. The island decorations were very elaborate, and she laughed when she found out that the "Fun Shack" was actually the trunk Jenna had arrived in.

After everyone had admired Natalie's bedroom (and all the pictures of her with movie stars and other celebrities), Natalie broke out more sodas and snacks. Alex had some bottled water. She was relieved to see that Natalie had made sure to provide lots of veggies and cheese. One condition of her coming to the overnight was that she would eat carefully.

Natalie gave everyone some ground rules and explained that they would keep the sodas in the fridge, with spares to restock as they drank the cold ones. Then they talked about the reunion for a long time. Alex got teased big-time about Adam and Peter both. She didn't mind. It was actually kind of fun to get teased about boys!

After a while, they moved on to other things, and Alex had a sense that the sleepover was officially beginning, just the way Dr. Steve had announced that the party at Village Bowl had just begun.

"Okay! Alyssa has made something really special for everybody," Natalie announced as her guests arranged their suitcases and sleeping bags in the living room.

Alyssa stood up while Natalie and Jenna walked to a pile of what looked like canvas tote bags. Natalie picked one up and handed it to Alyssa.

Alyssa showed it to the girls. There was a moon, a star, and a pine tree, and the words CAMP LAKEVIEW REUNION BUNK 3C in a semicircle. "I designed the logo, and Natalie's mom got twelve bags made," Alyssa explained, as the others ooh'ed and aah'ed.

Then Grace and Natalie passed out the bags.

"Mine's smeared. No surprise there," Chelsea muttered as she examined the front of her bag.

Alex looked over at it. Sure enough, the moon and the star had run together, and the letters were smudged.

"Oh, I'm sorry! I didn't notice," Natalie said, reaching for it. "I'll trade with you."

Chelsea firmly held it in her lap. "It's okay. I'm not going to use it anyway," she snapped.

There was an awkward moment. Natalie said, "I can get my mom to make you another one."

"Natalie, *hello?*" Chelsea said angrily. "*I said it's fine.*"

"Okay, then. Moving right along." Grace cleared her throat as she stood up. "Welcome to the Camp Lakeview Book Club. I am your fearless book club leader. My two assistants will now pass out notebooks and pencils. And then we'll have a little quiz."

"I think I'm going to get another soda," Jessie announced.

"And I have to use the bathroom," Sarah said. "Go ahead and start without me."

Grace blinked, a little thrown. Natalie and Alyssa passed out small notebooks and pencils to six of the girls sitting cross-legged on the floor: Candace, Alex, Natalie, Alyssa, Chelsea, and Brynn. Natalie didn't know where Karen had gone.

Grace rustled her papers. "Okay. These are questions about famous books, okay? The first section is titles. First question. This book is about adult females who are about three inches tall. What's the title of it?"

Alex got it right away. She chuckled. Beside her, Brynn muttered, "*What?*"

"Are these supposed to be trick questions?" Chelsea demanded.

Alex said, "I got it!"

"You would. You're such a brain," Chelsea grumbled.

Ignore it, be nice to her, Alex reminded herself. "Thanks," she told Chelsea. She said to Grace, "It's *Little Women*."

"Bing!" Grace imitated a bell. "That's correct!"

"That was too hard," Chelsea groaned.

"Okay." Grace pushed on, reading off the next clue. "This book is about the god of jewelry."

The girls frowned at Grace. Not one pencil moved. This time Alex was stumped, too.

"*The Lord of the Rings!*" Grace smiled weakly. "Get it?"

Chelsea rolled her eyes and shook her head.

Grace looked down at her list. Brynn shifted restlessly. Natalie stifled a yawn.

"And that's all the time we have for the Book Club Quiz!" Grace said, flinging open her arms.

"Yay!" Chelsea cried.

Alex winced at Chelsea's rudeness. She could see that Grace had prepared a lot more questions, and that she had stopped the quiz early. She was probably disappointed that it hadn't gone very well.

As if Grace had read her mind, she winked at Alex and wadded up the papers into a ball. She tossed it into the air a couple of times and said, "Time for a soda."

"I'll get you one," Alex offered.

"Cream soda, please," Grace said. "And thanks!"

"You're welcome," Alex said warmly as she got up and walked into the kitchen.

Natalie and Alyssa caught up with her.

"I'm trying so hard to be nice to you-know-who," Natalie said to her two friends as they got the sodas. "But it's really difficult."

"I know," Alyssa said. "I'm afraid to say anything. She takes it all wrong."

Natalie popped open a root beer. She leaned against the counter and took a sip. "I just want to stay in here for, like an hour. I'm totally on edge. It seems like the nicer we are to her, the meaner she acts."

"I know," Alex said. "It's nerve-wracking."

"But we have to be nice," Alyssa reminded them. "No matter what."

"You're right," Natalie said. She took another sip of root beer and sighed. "Well, I can't hide out in my kitchen during my own sleepover. I should go back out there."

"No, you can't hide, but you can take a moment to regroup," Alyssa said loyally. "You're under a lot of pressure, Nat. And whether she means to be a pain or not, Chelsea's not helping," she added.

"You guys are really sweet," Natalie told them, giving them both big hugs.

The three friends walked back into the living room. Chelsea glared at them and said, "Secrets are not cool at sleepovers."

Natalie's face tingled. Feeling guilty, she said, "No secrets, Chelsea." She looked around the room at the rest of the bunk. People seemed unsure what to do next. "Hey, why don't we all get our sleeping bags out and change into our pajamas? Then we can relax."

"It'll be good to relax," Candace said.

Jessie and Karen walked over to the pile of sleeping bags. Chelsea waited a moment, and then she did, too.

As Chelsea approached, Karen looked nervous. She was hugging her sleeping bag, and Natalie wondered if she didn't want to sleep next to Chelsea. The other girls were standing around, too, as if no one wanted to be the first one to put down their bag.

"We're going to be crammed together," Karen said, sliding a glance toward Chelsea. That confirmed it for Natalie: Karen wanted some space—literally—between herself and Chelsea.

"Crammed," Candace agreed.

"Why don't you sleep next to me, Chelsea?" Sarah offered.

"Or me," Natalie said quickly.

Pretty soon everyone was half-fighting to get Chelsea to sleep next to them. It had to be obvious that they were being overly nice.

"Just so long as no one has BO or bad breath," Chelsea drawled as she held onto her bag with one hand and fanned her face with the other. "I mean, it was bad enough at camp, inhaling everybody's stinky foot odor, and we had lots of room between our bunks. Got any room deodorizer, Natalie? Because we sure need some!"

Jenna dropped her sleeping bag on the floor.

"I have had it with you!" Jenna cried.

She stomped over to her laptop, picked it up, glared at Chelsea, and hit a button. Gaby's recorded voice filled the room.

"Knock it off! Knock it off!"

Chelsea gasped. So did everyone else.

Chelsea dropped her sleeping back and raced out of the living room, down the hall, and into the guest bathroom. The door slammed shut and the stupid motion-detector singing fish began to warble. The sound overlaid Jenna's laptop as it continued to blare, "Knock it off! Knock it off!"

"Turn it off!" Natalie implored.

"I'm trying! I'm trying!" Jenna cried. She frantically punched buttons, but nothing happened.

Anxiously, Jenna put the laptop into the "Fun Shack" and closed the trunk lid. It only served to muffle the sound a little.

"Knock it off! Knock it off!"

Jenna tried to open the trunk back up. "It's locked!" she cried.

"Get the key!" Natalie told her.

"There is no key!" Jenna rattled the handle. "We lost it on our family vacation to Idaho!"

"Oh, great. Then let's get it out of here," Grace told her. She pulled the decorations off the trunk and began to push it out of the living room. Jenna assisted her, guiding the wheels over the carpet.

"Put it in the kitchen," Jessie suggested.

Natalie put out her hands. "Or in my mom's office. Then we can at least shut the door!"

While Grace and Sarah handled that, Jenna said to Natalie, "I have got to go apologize to Chelsea. I feel so stupid. I just lost it."

"I'll come with you," Natalie offered. "I'll turn off the fish." She said to Alex, "You guys get Chelsea's present ready, okay? We'll get her to come out and then we'll give it to her."

"Got it," Alex said.

Natalie and Jenna hurried together to the bathroom door. Their approach signaled the fish to flap and sing all over again, until Natalie hit the "off" switch. Then she knocked softly on the door.

"Chelsea?" she called. "It's Natalie."

"And Jenna. I'm so sorry!" Jenna said through the door. "It was supposed to be a joke!"

"You are so lying, Jenna Bloom." Chelsea's voice was muffled. She sounded as if she were crying.

"Please come out," Natalie said. "We have something for you."

"Uh-huh, what is it, a ride home?" Chelsea snapped.

"No, it's something we made," Natalie assured her.

"And we made it for you. All of us."

"Another thing you did behind my back! You just love doing stuff like that, don't you, Natalie? It makes you feel really important."

Natalie flushed. She turned to Jenna. "I don't know what to do."

Jenna made a face. "Your mom's coming home at midnight, right?"

"Oh, we can't spend the whole sleepover like this!" Natalie cried. She knocked a little more loudly on the door. "Chelsea, please come out!"

"Go away!" Chelsea cried. "Go away and leave me alone!"

Natalie was stumped. What were they going to do?

chapter

THIRTEEN

What a disaster! Alex thought as she faced her bunkmates and everyone just kind of stared at one another. Grace and Sarah had wheeled the trunk with the laptop into Ms. Goode's office, but she could still hear it faintly saying, "Knock it off! Knock it off!"

She wondered how long it would be until the battery ran out.

"What should we do?" Karen asked her.

Alex thought a moment. Finally she said, "We all know that Chelsea is upset about her dad."

"Because he's sick and stuff," Jessie said.

"Yes." Alex nodded.

"Which is why she's acting like a total jerk," Grace huffed.

"Yes." Alex nodded again. Then she thought back to when she had gone into diabetic shock at camp.

Chelsea had been the one to stand by her. It had been Chelsea who had rushed off to get her insulin kit. And Chelsea who had told them that she had a cousin who had juvenile diabetes, and what a horrible disease it was.

Alex had been grateful not only that she had physically helped her, but that Chelsea, alone of all her bunkmates, understood that having diabetes was really awful. Chelsea was the one who had talked about it the most honestly, instead of just trying to cheer Alex up.

"She's not getting a chance to talk about it," Alex said slowly, beginning to understand. "She's been acting really bad, and we've been ignoring it because we feel sorry for her."

"That's right," Grace snapped. She narrowed her eyes and crossed her hands over her chest. "We have totally been letting her get away with it."

"That's not what she wants," Alex told her.

As Natalie and Jenna walked back into the living room, Alex addressed them all.

"Through the summer, and leading up to now, each one of us has had a problem. And the others have tried to pitch in and *help*. We're just putting up with Chelsea. We're not helping her."

Candace opened her arms wide. "But she won't *let* us help her," she said.

"I know about being sick," Alex said. "I know she's scared." Alex looked at each bunkmate in turn. "She has a right to be scared. Things might not go well for her dad. There's no way to know."

"I get it," Natalie said. "Chelsea needs to be *heard*. We've all been so busy trying to act like she's not being a totally rude jerk or cheering her up that Chelsea hasn't had a chance to be one of us—a bunkmate who needs her friends."

Alex raised a staying hand, then walked alone to

the bathroom door. She knocked softly and said, "Chelsea, it's me, Alex. I'm alone. May I come in?"

After a few seconds, the door slowly opened.

Chelsea stood in front of Alex. It was obvious she had been crying. But she kept her mouth pursed in a tight line and stared hard at Alex.

Swallowing, Alex said, "We're really sorry about your dad. Whatever happens, we're here for you. You're part of Bunk 3C, and we care about you."

Chelsea remained silent. But she didn't go back into the bathroom.

Alex walked her back to the living room. Everyone was standing—Grace, Natalie, Brynn, Jenna, Karen, Candace, Jessie, Alyssa, and Sarah.

Brynn was holding their gift for Chelsea, a large object about the size of two school notebooks and three times as thick. It was wrapped in sparkly pink paper.

"This is for you," Brynn said, holding it out to Chelsea.

Chelsea hesitated. "What is it?"

"Open it and see," Natalie urged her, stepping toward her.

Studying the faces of her bunkmates, Chelsea reached out and took the present. As she slowly unwrapped it, Brynn explained, "We made this for you because we care about you. Not to go behind your back."

As Chelsea tore the paper away, the gift was revealed. It was a large scrapbook-style journal, with *Chelsea's Book* written in silver gel pen on the black cover.

"What . . . ?" Chelsea said, her voice cracking.

Brynn sat her down. "It's a journal for recording

your thoughts," she said. "And expressing your feelings, and remembering that you're not alone in all this."

As Chelsea turned the pages, Natalie took up the thread. "We personalized it just for you. There are pictures of all of us at camp, and essays about different things we wanted to share with you."

"I wrote a haiku," Alyssa said.

"I made a magazine collage," Natalie added.

"Oh my God," Chelsea murmured as she kept looking through the journal. There were photos and pictures cut out of magazines, arranged into intricate collages. Tiny envelopes held little notes, and stickers of flowers and angels decorated the borders of each page.

Chelsea's eyes welled with tears. "You guys worked so hard on this. For . . . *me*."

"Yes. For you," Alex concluded.

Chelsea broke down. Weeping, she covered her face with her hands. Grace opened her mouth to speak, but Alex touched her arm and shook her head.

"When he got sick the first time," Chelsea said hoarsely, "I was so . . . I was *mad*. I wanted to be like you guys, worrying about nail polish and horoscopes and boys, but what if he . . . then he got sick again . . . and I didn't know what to do. I still don't know what to do!"

Chelsea cried and cried. And the girls of Bunk 3C cried with her, and each one in turn held her tightly.

"We hear you," Alex told her. "And we're here for you."

▲ ▲ ▲

By the time Natalie's mother came home, Chelsea

had joined the party—for the first time ever, really. She was wearing a long nightgown with Exeter Academy—the name of her boarding school—in a shield on the front. All the girls were in their pj's, yakking and laughing. Five girls—Grace, Jenna, Alyssa, Brynn, and Candace—were watching the first movie Natalie's father had ever been in. It was a really bad, low-budget horror movie. They were laughing so hard, they couldn't sit up straight.

"Hi, Mom," Natalie sang out. Seated on the back of the couch, she was cradling the most recent issue of *YM* in her lap. The other five bunkmates—Alex, Sarah, Jessie, Chelsea, and Karen—were sitting on the carpet, which was protected by pages from the *New York Times*, while they painted their nails.

"Okay, how many vote for the perfume personality quiz?" Natalie asked.

Alex, Sarah, and Chelsea raised their hands.

"Off the back of the couch please, Nat," her mom said.

Natalie scooted down. "Did you have a nice evening?" she asked her mom. Then, before her mom could answer, she asked the girls, "Okay, how many want to hear their horoscopes?"

Jessie and Karen raised their hands. Chelsea did, too.

"Chelsea!" Alex protested. "You can't vote twice!"

"Sure I can!" Chelsea insisted, laughing.

The five girls laughed as hard as the ones who were watching the movie.

"Yes, I did. Anything I need to know about?" Natalie's mom asked, sounding amused.

"It's all good," Natalie told her.

"Well, I'm glad you ladies are having fun," Natalie's mom said. "I'll say good night."

"Night, Mom!" Natalie called, still laughing.

Her mother left the room. About ten seconds later, she reappeared.

"What is Jenna's trunk doing in my office?"

Natalie covered her mouth. "We forgot!"

She looked at the crazy mob of girls sprawled all over her living room. It seemed like forever ago that they had stashed the trunk in her mom's office.

"You forgot why it's there or you forgot to take it out?" her mom asked. "Never mind. We'll take care of it tomorrow."

"Thanks, Mom," Natalie said. Her eyes shone. "This is the best sleepover ever!"

"You got that right!" Grace boomed.

Everyone cheered.

"Girls! Not so loud! It's midnight!" Natalie's mom admonished them. But she looked really happy.

Almost as happy as Natalie herself!

▲ ▲ ▲

Everyone slept late on Sunday morning. Then Hannah called to tell Natalie that it was nice to meet all her camp girlfriends.

Then she cleared her throat and said, "May I speak to Alyssa? You can stay on."

Alyssa got on the extension. Hannah said, "I think you and I got off on the wrong foot. Maybe you and I don't have much in common besides Natalie. But she's an excellent friend to each of us. Am I right?"

"You are right," Alyssa said. "Thanks, Hannah."

"Cool," Hannah said, and hung up.

Alyssa smiled at Natalie. "You've got an excellent friend, Nat."

Natalie grinned at her. "Yes, I do. In fact, I've got two!"

Natalie's mom treated everybody to a proper New York breakfast at Mavin Deli. She ordered piles of blueberry and cranberry bagels, and two large carafes of hot chocolate. Chelsea laughed at everyone's silly jokes and then they all hung their spoons on their noses just like the dorky boys in Simon and Adam's bunk. Natalie's mom just shook her head and smiled.

They finished their tasty breakfast and loped through Central Park. It had snowed during the night, and the large, naturally landscaped park in the center of New York City glittered and gleamed. Despite the fact that they weren't dressed for rough-and-tumble play, the girls plunged into powdery snowdrifts and threw snowballs at one another, whooping with glee.

"We're all going to have to go soon," Alyssa said, panting, as they took a break. "We have buses to catch, parents coming . . ."

"I can't believe our Camp Lakeview reunion weekend is almost over," Natalie told her. "You were so awesome. You helped me so much. Thank you."

"You're welcome, Nat. Of course," Alyssa said.

They hugged.

Then Natalie shouted, "Everybody, come here! Mom!" She held out her digital camera. "Take our picture, please?"

Her mother had stood off to one side, giving the girls some room to roam. Now she strode over to Natalie and took the camera from her.

"Okay, girls of 3C," Natalie's mom said, backing away as she looked through the viewfinder. "Everyone scoot in tight!"

Snow began to fall as they put their arms on one another's shoulders. Chelsea stood in the middle of the first row, a girl on either side of her hanging onto her, and she holding onto them.

"Say 3C!" Grace shouted.

"3C!" everyone bellowed, grinning at the camera.

"Hi, Valerie!" Alex shouted.

Everyone yelled, "Hi, Valerie!"

"Hey! This snow tastes like Twizzlers!" Chelsea cried.

At the exact same time, everyone tipped back their heads.

"It does!" Natalie cried.

"It totally does!" Alex yelled.

"Well! This is going to make a strange picture!" Natalie's mom protested.

"It's going to be an excellent picture!" Natalie corrected her.

"You got that right!" Grace cried.

The bunkmates cheered and hooted.

They were the girls of Bunk 3C, truly together at last.

Turn the page for a sneak preview of

camp CONFIDENTIAL

Second Summer

Second Time's the Charm

available soon!

Get ready—the summer is hotter
the second time around!

chapter ONE

Dear Hannah:

I guess sometimes the truth really is stranger than fiction, huh? Or, the more things change the more they stay the same. Or even, a rolling stone gathers no moss? Whatever, I'm babbling, and you can feel free to insert your own cliché HERE. The point is that if this time last year you had told me that I would be RETURNING to Camp Lake-puke—voluntarily, no less—I would have laughed in your face. And then run away crying.

And yet. Here I am, crowded onto a smelly, oversized charter bus and surrounded by kids singing "99 Bottles of Beer on the Wall" at the top of their lungs. And even though they are only at 87 bottles, and even though some of these kids couldn't even make the first cut of "American Idol," I don't have the vaguest impulse to scream. In fact, I'm feeling pretty zen. I even chimed in for a bar or two, somewhere back around 81 bottles or so.

Pretty amazing, huh?

Not only am I not hating the thought of coming back to camp, but I'm even sort of excited about it. Mom shipped me out with a survival kit of soy chips and Powerbars well in advance this time around. No more tuna surprises for me! And I am all stocked up on magazines. Alyssa's here sitting next to me—she says hi—and Grace is somewhere up front, leading a small faction of non-singers in a rousing game of bus charades. It's hilarious. And I can't wait to see the rest of the girls: Jenna, Valerie, Sarah, Alex, and the other 3C-ers.

And, um, a particular boy.

Yes, Simon. He's been awesome about writing and calling, as you know, but we've only seen each other once in person since the reunion. I'm going into serious withdrawal. I really, really hope he's as excited to see me as I am to see him. But only time will tell, right?

Right. I wish you were here to give me one of your patented pep talks.

In case you haven't noticed, I'm a little nervous.

Anyway, the natives are getting restless, which must mean that we're almost there. That, and Alyssa just told me that we're almost there. See how smart I am?

I'd better sign off. Try not to miss me too much while you're strolling along the Champs Elysées, eating chocolate croissants and shopping till you drop. You can feel free to send me some French truffles whenever the spirit moves you.

Write soon,

Natalie

Natalie Goode capped her purple felt-tipped pen, folded her letter to her best friend, Hannah, into quarters, and tucked it into the front pouch of her backpack. She sighed contentedly. Hannah was spending the summer in France with her mother, a superglamorous foreign ambassador. Hannah's parents traveled a ton for work, and over the summers they preferred to travel *with* their daughter, generally to various exotic locales.

Not Natalie's parents, though. Natalie's mother was an art buyer, and summers were her time to scout new talent. And Natalie's father . . . well, he had a pretty offbeat career.

Natalie's father was Tad Maxwell, a hugely famous movie star who mostly appeared in big-time action movies. He lived in L.A. full-time but was on the road a lot, shooting on location and doing press junkets for his various movies and stuff. Natalie missed him, of course, but her parents had gotten divorced when she was pretty young and so she was used to the situation by now. Her dad loved her; she knew that beyond a doubt, and she never took the time that they had together for granted.

In fact, for Natalie, the biggest thing about having a famous father was worrying what other kids would think of her. At her school, lots of kids had parents who were ultra-wealthy or had high-powered jobs and stuff. So they didn't think anything of the fact that Natalie's father was a movie star. But she never knew how other people—and in particular, new people—would react.

That was one of the reasons Natalie had been so nervous last summer, when her mother had sent her off to Camp Lakeview—or "Lake-puke," as Nat had affectionately come to call it (the other reason had to do with a deathly aversion to "the Great Outdoors" that Nat had since gotten over, thankfully).

When Natalie thought about how totally unenthusiastic she had been about camp last summer, she had to laugh. After all, she'd made some amazing friends at Lakeview, and learned a lot about herself in the process. Okay, sure, people were *slightly* weirded out when they found out the truth about her father, but her friends—her real friends—were mostly just disappointed that she hadn't felt that she could confide in them. And besides, that was all over, now, anyway, Her secret was out in the open. *Way* out in open. Natalie wondered if her friend Alex, a Lakeview legacy and soccer champ, brought her Tad Maxwell poster back to camp this summer. *Or maybe she even got a new one*, Nat thought. Alex could be a little bit of a know-it-all, but she was a dedicated camper and a supremely loyal friend. Natalie was psyched to be bunking with her again this summer.

"I can't wait to see Jenna," Alyssa said, rousing Natalie from her internal monologue. "She told me she bought a book of practical jokes that she's dying to try out."

"Jenna should know better than that," Natalie quipped. Their fellow 3C-er was a noted prankster whose jokes had not gone without consequence the summer before. Of course, her good humor was so infectious that it was difficult to stay upset with her for too long.

"Anyway, she told me that she would meet us at the great field, where the buses let out," Alyssa continued. She pointed out the streaky tinted window. "Can you see her?" she asked, cupping her head against the glass and squinting outward. Their bus was, at present, rumbling to a halt along the field. Somehow, while Natalie had been lost in her daydream, they had arrived at camp!

"Yeah, she's . . ." Natalie's voice trailed off as she broke out laughing. "She's the one tap-dancing down the path. Minus the tap shoes." She giggled again as their friend made her way into the melee of the great field, kicking up great clouds of dust as she moved forward.

Their bus screeched to a halt, coughing exhaust fumes and sputtering as the engine died. The campers cried out, jumping out of their seats and moving eagerly toward the door. "One at a time," their bus counselor, Pete, begged in vain. Pete was a member of the kitchen staff who was so good-natured that it was hard to hold his terrible cooking against him.

"I call top bunk," Natalie shouted, playfully shoving past Alyssa and bounding down the steps of the bus.

"Hey, no fair calling the bunk before it's in sight," Alyssa protested, hot on Natalie's heels.

"Jenna!" Natalie shrieked, flinging her arms

around her friend as though they hadn't seen each other in ages. *Which, come to think of it, we haven't,* Natalie realized. The last time their entire bunk had been together had been at the camp reunion—back in February! "Did you see our bunk yet? Is it nicer than last year's bunk? Is there mold in the showers? Are the screen windows torn?" The perma-smile faded from Jenna's face, prompting Natalie's suspicion. "Oh, no. *Is* there mold in the showers?"

Jenna shook her head slowly. She wasn't tap-dancing anymore. Natalie had a feeling that whatever Jenna had to tell her, it was pretty serious. "Uh-oh," Natalie teased, trying to lighten the mood. "Are there *spiders* in the showers?"

Jenna smiled, but it was a weak smile, at best. *This has got to be bad news,* Natalie thought, a cold fist of dread settling into her stomach like a lead weight.

Alyssa, always no-nonsense, adjusted her tote bag over her shoulder and stepped forward, hands on her hips like she meant business. "Come on, Jenna? Worse than spiders? Spill."

"It's 4C," Jenna said, looking much more somber than Natalie could ever recall seeing her.

"What, did we get, like, an awful counselor or something?" Natalie asked, growing increasingly worried.

"Well, no. At least, most of us didn't," Jenna said, nervously. "It's just . . ."

Natalie raised her eyebrow quizzically.

"Our bunk!" Jenna finally blurted. "We're not all

together this summer."

"You mean . . ." Alyssa cut in anxiously.

"Exactly," Jenna said, shaking her head. "We've been split up!"